NOT GEORGE WASHINGTON

"NOT GEORGE WASHINGTON "

An Autobiographical Novel

P. G. Wodehouse and Herbert Westbrook

Edited and Introduced by
DAVID A. JASEN

c/

CONTINUUM · New York

1980
The Continuum Publishing Corporation
815 Second Avenue, New York, N.Y.   10017

Printed in the United States of America
Designed by Victoria Gomez

Library of Congress Cataloging in Publication Data

Wodehouse, Pelham Grenville, 1881–1975.
Not George Washington.

"A Continuum book."
I. Westbrook, Herbert, joint author.   II. Jasen,
David A.   III. Title.
PZ3.W817Nn   [PR6045.053]   823′9′12   79-24168
ISBN 0-8264-0006-x

CONTENTS

Introduction by
DAVID A. JASEN

Although *Not George Washington* was written in 1906 and published in England the following year, it has never appeared in the United States. For Wodehouse fans, this novel should prove a real treat. It is not only a good story (told in the manner that Wilkie Collins made famous in *The Moonstone,* that of having more than one narrator to tell the tale), but is filled with bits of autobiography.

Unlike his hero, James Orlebar Cloyster, who was known as James, Wodehouse, whose given name was Pelham, was called Plum by family and friends almost from the beginning. But Plum and Cloyster shared many events and attitudes, chief being the desire, nay, compulsion to make a living by writing. Writing anything and everything, as a peek into the Wodehouse diary at the end of 1904 shows: "On this, the 13th of December, 1904, time 12 p.m., I set it down that I have *arrived*. Letter from Cosmo Hamilton congratulating me on my work and promising commission to write lyrics for his next piece. I have a lyric in 'Sergeant Brue,' a serial in *The Captain,* 5 books published, I am editing 'By the Way,' *Pearson's* have two stories and two poems of mine, I have finished the 'Kid Brady' stories, and I have a commission to do a weekly poem for *Vanity Fair.*"

When Plum left school to live in London in the fall of 1900, his first residence consisted of a small bed-sitting-room in Markham Square which he described as "horrible lodgings in the Chelsea neighborhood off the King's Road." It was here he amassed his large collection of rejection slips but met with occasional success, as in November, 1900, when his first humorous article, "Men Who Missed Their Own Weddings," was published in *Tit-Bits.*

As a result of his reading James M. Barrie's novel *When a Man's Single*—whose hero, a young man like Plum who was endeavoring to become a journalist, was urged to write to please editors rather than to please himself—Plum took the advice therein and planned a campaign to bombard editors with his articles, poems, and short stories.

Upon learning that an ex-schoolmaster of his was working for an evening newspaper *The Globe,* he went to see him to ask if he could get him some work. William Beach-Thomas, who had given up teaching in favor of journalism, was assistant to Harold Begbie, editor of *The Globe*'s "By the Way" feature column. As Beach-Thomas and Begbie often wanted to take a day off, they were glad to have Plum fill in for them. Eventually, Plum became editor of the column and ran it for five years.

Early in 1903, Plum moved to a more salubrious part of Chelsea, sparsely furnishing the large top room at 23 Walpole Street where, on a cold winter's night, he received a visitor. Herbert W. Westbrook arrived with a letter of introduction from a mutual friend to find Plum sitting at a table (his only one), a woollen sweater wrapped around his feet, working on a poem for

Punch by the light of a green-shaded oil lamp (again, his only one). Westbrook recalled that "Plum gave me some good advice and, more than that, sincere encouragement." Westbrook, in turn, invited Plum to stay at Emsworth House—a small preparatory school in the country, at which Westbrook was an assistant master—where the atmosphere would be conducive to writing. Eventually, Plum took Westbrook on as his assistant for the "By the Way" column.

Westbrook was an eccentric, some of whose antics are told in *P. G. Wodehouse: A Portrait of a Master.* The plot of *Not George Washington,* as well as the plot for the short story "Rallying Round Old George," were supplied by Westbrook. But, Plum did the actual writing of both. As Plum is a thinly disguised Cloyster, so too is Westbrook easily discernible as Julian Eversleigh. Westbrook/Eversleigh's slothfulness is playfully pointed to in Plum's dedication of a public school novel "To that Prince of Slackers, Herbert Westbrook."

By the start of 1906, Plum had an offer from Sir Seymour Hicks, actor-manager of the Aldwych Theatre, to be the resident lyric and verse writer for all the Aldwych shows. "On leaving the stage-door," reported Westbrook after the initial heady experience, "Plum was so stunned with joy and excitement that we walked a mile along the Strand without him knowing where he was or whether he was coming or going." Thus Plum embarked on his life-long love affair with the theatre. And, like Cloyster, Plum had his first big song hit "Mr. Chamberlain," in his first show for Hicks. The composer was the fledgling American tunesmith Jerome Kern.

The plot of *Not George Washington* concerns an author who submits for publication many different types of material under the names of various nonliterary acquaintances to each of whom he pays a percentage of his earnings for such usage. Here the main theme is carried to an interesting and amusing extreme, but it obviously had its origins in the actual experiences of the two authors. That they did this sort of thing is clearly seen in a short note appearing in Plum's diary for January 1907: "I wrote this [article] under H. Westbrook's name. We divided the gns. Clever work."

Let us enjoy the young author on his way to fame and fortune as he pulls out yet another plum.

Part One

Miss Margaret Goodwin's Narrative

Chapter 1

JAMES ARRIVES

I am Margaret Goodwin. A week from today I shall be Mrs. James Orlebar Cloyster.

It is just three years since I first met James. We made each other's acquaintance at half-past seven on the morning of the 28th of July in the middle of Fermain Bay, about fifty yards from the shore.

Fermain Bay is in Guernsey. My home had been with my mother for many years at St. Martin's in that island. There we two lived our uneventful lives until fate brought one whom, when first I set my eyes on him, I knew I loved.

Perhaps it is indiscreet of me to write that down. But what does it matter? It is for no one's reading but my own. James, my *fiancé*, is *not* peeping slyly over my shoulder as I write. On the contrary, my door is locked, and James is, I believe, in the smoking-room of his hotel at St. Peter's Port.

At that time it had become my habit to begin my day by rising before breakfast and taking a swim in Fermain Bay, which lies across the road in front of our cottage. The practice—I have since abandoned it—was good for the complexion, and generally healthy. I had kept it up, moreover, because I had somehow cherished an unreasonable but persistent presentiment that some day Somebody (James, as it turned out) would cross the pathway of my maiden existence. I told myself that I must be ready for him. It would never do for him to arrive, and find no one to meet him.

On the 28th of July I started off as usual. I wore a short tweed skirt, brown stockings—my ankles were, and are, good—a calico blouse, and a red tam-o'-shanter. Ponto barked at my heels. In one hand I carried my blue twill bathing-gown. In the other a miniature alpenstock. The sun had risen sufficiently to scatter the slight mist of the summer morning, and a few flecked clouds were edged with a slender frame of red gold.

Leisurely, and with my presentiment strong upon me, I descended the steep cliffside to the cave on the left of the bay, where, guarded by the faithful Ponto, I was accustomed to disrobe; and soon afterwards I came out, my dark hair over my shoulders and blue twill over a portion of the rest of me, to climb out to the point of the projecting rocks, so that I might dive gracefully and safely into the still blue water.

I was a good swimmer. I reached the ridge on the opposite side of the bay without fatigue, not changing from a powerful breast-stroke. I then sat for a while at the water's edge to rest and to drink in the thrilling glory of what my heart persisted in telling me was the morning of my life.

And then I saw Him.

Not distinctly, for he was rowing a dinghy in my direction, and consequently had his back to me.

In the stress of my emotions and an aggravation of modesty, I dived again. With an intensity like that of a captured conger I yearned to be hidden by the water. I could watch him as I swam, for, strictly speaking, he was in my way, though a little farther out to sea than I intended to go. As I drew near, I noticed that he wore an odd garment like a dressing-gown. He had stopped rowing.

I turned upon my back for a moment's rest, and, as I did so, heard a cry. I resumed my former attitude, and brushed the salt water from my eyes.

The dinghy was wobbling unsteadily. The dressing-gown was in the bows; and he, my sea-god, was in the water. Only for a second I saw him. Then he sank.

How I blessed the muscular development of my arms.

I reached him as he came to the surface.

"That's twice," he remarked contemplatively, as I seized him by the shoulders.

"Be brave," I said excitedly; "I can save you."

"I should be most awfully obliged," he said.

"Do exactly as I tell you."

"I say," he remonstrated, "you're not going to drag me along by the roots of my hair, are you?"

The natural timidity of man is, I find, attractive.

I helped him to the boat, and he climbed in. I trod water, clinging with one hand to the stern.

"Allow me," he said, bending down.

"No, thank you," I replied.

"Not, really?"

"Thank you very much, but I think I will stay where I am."

"But you may get cramp. By the way—I'm really frightfully obliged to you for saving my life—I mean, a perfect stranger—I'm afraid it's quite spoiled your dip."

"Not at all," I said politely. "Did you get cramp?"

"A twinge. It was awfully kind of you."

"Not at all."

Then there was a rather awkward silence.

"Is this your first visit to Guernsey?" I asked.

"Yes; I arrived yesterday. It's a delightful place. Do you live here?"

"Yes; that white cottage you can just see through the trees."

"I suppose I couldn't give you a tow anywhere?"

"No; thank you very much. I will swim back."

Another constrained silence.

"Are you ever in London, Miss——?"

"Goodwin. Oh, yes; we generally go over in the winter, Mr.——"

"Cloyster. Really? How jolly. Do you go to the theatre much?"

"Oh, yes. We saw nearly everything last time we were over."

There was a third silence. I saw a remark about the weather trembling on his lip, and, as I was beginning to feel the chill of the water a little, I determined to put a temporary end to the conversation.

"I think I will be swimming back now," I said.

"You're quite sure I can't give you a tow?"

"Quite, thanks. Perhaps you would care to come to breakfast with us, Mr. Cloyster? I know my mother would be glad to see you."

"It is very kind of you. I should be delighted. Shall we meet on the beach?"

I swam off to my cave to dress.

Breakfast was a success, for my mother was a philosopher. She said very little, but what she did say was magnificent. In her youth she had moved in literary circles, and now found her daily pleasure in the works of Schopenhauer, Kant, and other Germans. Her lightest reading was *Sartor Resartus,* and occasionally she would drop into Ibsen and Maeterlinck, the asparagus of her philosophic banquet. Her chosen mode of thought, far from leaving her inhuman or intolerant, gave her a social distinction which I had inherited from her. I could, if I had wished it, have attended with success the tea-drinkings, the tennis-playings, and the éclair-and-lemonade dances to which I was frequently invited. But I always refused. Nature was my hostess. Nature, which provided me with balmy zephyrs that were more comforting than buttered toast; which set the race of the waves to the ridges of Fermain, where arose no shrill, heated voice crying, "Love—forty"; which decked foliage in more splendid sheen than anything the local costumier could achieve, and whose poplars swayed more rhythmically than the dancers of the Assembly Rooms.

The constraint which had been upon us during our former conversation vanished at breakfast. We were both hungry, and we had a common topic. We related our story of the sea in alternate sentences. We ate and we talked, turn and turn about. My mother listened. To her the affair, compared with the tremendous subjects to which she was accustomed to direct her mind, was broad farce. James took it with an air of restrained amusement. I, seriously.

Tentatively, I diverged from this subject towards other and wider fields. Impressions of Guernsey, which drew from him his address, at the St. Peter's Port Hotel. The horrors of the sea passage from Weymouth, which extorted a comment on the limitations of England. England. London. Kensington. South Kensington. The Gunton-Cresswells? Yes, yes! Extraordinary. Curious coincidence. Excursus on smallness of world. Queer old gentleman, Mr. Gunton-Cresswell. He is, indeed. Quite one of the old school. Oh, quite. Still wears that beaver hat? Does he really? Yes. Ha, ha! Yes.

Here the humanising influence of the Teutonic school of philosophic analysis was demonstrated by my mother's action. Mr. Cloyster, she said, must reconcile himself to exchanging his comfortable rooms at the St. Peter's Port—("I particularly dislike half-filled hotel life, Mrs. Goodwin")—for the shelter of our cottage. He accepted. He was then "warned" that I was chef at the cottage. Mother gave him "a chance to change his mind." Something was said about my saving life and destroying digestion. He went to collect his things in an ecstasy of merriment.

At this point I committed an indiscretion which can only be excused by the magnitude of the occasion.

My mother had retired to her favourite bow-window where, by a *tour de force* on the part of the carpenter, a system of low, adjustable bookcases had been craftily constructed in such a way that when she sat in her window-seat they jutted in a semicircle towards her hand.

James, whom I had escorted down the garden path, had left me at the little wooden gate and had gone swinging down the road. I, shielded from outside observation (if any) by a line of lilacs, gazed rapturously at his retreating form. The sun was high in the sky now. It was a perfect summer's day. Birds were singing. Their notes blended with the gentle murmur of the sea on the beach below. Every fibre of my body was thrilling with the magic of the morning.

Through the kindly branches of the lilac I watched him, and then, as though in obedience to the primæval call of that July sunshine, I stood on tiptoe, and blew him a kiss.

I realised in an instant what I had done. Fool that I had been. The bow-window!

I was rigid with discomfiture. My mother's eyes were on the book she held. And yet a faint smile seemed to hover round her lips. I walked in silence to where she sat at the open window.

She looked up. Her smile was more pronounced.

"Margie," she said.

"Yes, mother?"

"The hedonism of Voltaire is the indictment of an honest bore."

"Yes, mother."

She then resumed her book.

Chapter 2

JAMES SETS OUT

(Miss Margaret Goodwin's narrative continued)

Those August days! Have there been any like them before? I realise with difficulty that the future holds in store for me others as golden.

The island was crammed with trippers. They streamed in by every boat. But James and I were infinitely alone. I loved him from the first, from the moment when he had rowed out of the unknown into my life, clad in a dressing-gown. I like to think that he loved me from that moment, too. But, if he did, the knowledge that he did came to him only after a certain delay. It was my privilege to watch this knowledge steal gradually but surely upon him.

We were always together; and as the days passed by he spoke freely of himself and his affairs, obeying unconsciously the rudder of my tactful inquisitiveness. By the end of the first week I knew as much about him as he did himself.

It seemed that a guardian—an impersonal sort of business man with a small but impossible family—was the most commanding figure in his private life. As for his finances, five-and-forty sovereigns, the remnant of a larger sum which had paid for his education at Cambridge, stood between him and the necessity of offering for hire a sketchy acquaintance with general literature and a third class in the classical tripos.

He had come to Guernsey to learn by personal observation what chances tomato growing held out to a young man in a hurry to get rich.

"Tomato growing?" I echoed dubiously. And then, to hide a sense of bathos, "People *have* made it pay. Of course, they work very hard."

"M'yes," said James without much enthusiasm.

"But I fancy," I added, "the life is not at all unpleasant."

At this point embarrassment seemed to engulf James. He blushed, swallowed once or twice in a somewhat convulsive manner, and stammered.

Then he made his confession guiltily.

I was not to suppose that his aims ceased with the attainment of a tomato-farm. The nurture of a wholesome vegetable occupied neither the whole of his ambitions nor even the greater part of them. To write—the agony with which he throatily confessed it!—to be swept into the maelstrom of literary journalism, to be *en rapport* with the unslumbering forces of Fleet Street—those were the real objectives of James Orlebar Cloyster.

"Of course, I mean," he said, "I suppose it would be a bit of a struggle at first, if you see what I mean. What I mean to say is, rejected manuscripts, and so on. But still, after a bit, once get a footing, you know—I should like to have a dash at it. I mean, I think I could do something, you know."

"Of course you could," I said.

"I mean, lots of men have, don't you know."

"There's plenty of room at the top," I said.

He seemed struck with this remark. It encouraged him.

He had had his opportunity of talking thus of himself during our long rambles out of doors. They were a series of excursions which he was accustomed to describe as hunting expeditions for the stocking of our larder.

Thus James would announce at breakfast that prawns were the day's quarry, and the foreshore round Cobo Bay the hunting-ground. And to Cobo, accordingly, we would set out. This prawn-yielding area extends along the coast on the other side of St. Peter's Port, where two halts had to be made, one at Madame Garnier's, the confectioners, the other at the library, to get fiction, which I never read. Then came a journey on the top of the antediluvian horse-tram, a sort of *diligence* on rails; and then a whole summer's afternoon among the prawns. Cobo is an expanse of shingle, dotted with seaweed and rocks; and Guernsey is a place where one can take off one's shoes and stockings on the slightest pretext. We waded hither and thither with the warm brine lapping unchecked over our bare legs. We did not use our nets very industriously, it is true; but our tongues were seldom still. The slow walk home was a thing to be looked forward to. Ah! those memorable homecomings in the quiet solemnity of that hour, when a weary sun stoops, one can fancy with a sigh of pleasure, to sink into the bosom of the sea!

Prawn-hunting was agreeably varied by fish-snaring, mussel-stalking, and mushroom-trapping—sports which James, in his capacity of Head Forester, included in his venery.

For mushroom-trapping an early start had to be made—usually between six and seven. The chase took us inland, until, after walking through the fragrant, earthy lanes, we turned aside into dewy meadows, where each blade of grass sparkled with a gem of purest water. Again the necessity of going barefoot.

Breakfast was late on these mornings, my mother whiling away the hours of waiting with a volume of Diogenes Laertius in the bow-window. She would generally open the meal with the remark that Anaximander held the primary cause of all things to be the Infinite, or that it was a favourite expression of Theophrastus that time was the most valuable thing a man could spend. When breakfast was announced, one of the covers concealed the mushrooms, which, under my superintendence, James had done his best to devil. A quiet day followed, devoted to sedentary recreation after the labours of the run.

The period which I have tried to sketch above may be called the period of good-fellowship. Whatever else love does for a woman, it makes her an actress. So we were merely excellent friends till James's eyes were opened. When that happened, he abruptly discarded good-fellowship. I, on the other hand, played it the more vigorously. The situation was mine.

Our day's run became the merest shadow of a formality. The office of Head Forester lapsed into an absolute sinecure. Love was with us—triumphant, and no longer to be skirted round by me; fresh, electric, glorious in James.

We talked—we must have talked. We moved. Our limbs performed their ordinary, daily movements. But a golden haze hangs over that second period. When, by the strongest effort of will, I can let my mind stand by those perfect moments, I seem to hear our voices, low and measured. And there are silences, fond in themselves and yet more fondly interrupted by unspoken messages from our eyes. What we really said, what we actually did, where precisely we two went, I do not know. We were together, and the blur of love was about us. Always the blur. It is not that memory cannot conjure up the scene again. It is not that the scene is clouded by the ill-proportion of a dream. No. It is because the dream is brought to me by will and not by sleep. The blur recurs because the blur was there. A love vast as ours is penalised, as it were, by this blur, which is the hall-mark of infinity.

In mighty distances, whether from earth to heaven, whether from 5245 Gerrard to 137 Glasgow, there is always that awful, that disintegrating blur.

A third period succeeded. I may call it the affectionately practical period. Instantly the blur vanishes. We were at our proper distance from the essence of things, and though infinity is something one yearns for passionately, one's normal condition has its meed of comfort. I remember once hearing a man in a Government office say that the pleasantest moment of his annual holiday was when his train rolled back into Paddington Station. And he was a man, too, of a naturally lazy disposition.

It was about the middle of this third period, during a mushroom-trapping ramble, that the idea occurred to us, first to me, then—after reflection—to James, that mother ought to be informed how matters stood between us.

We went into the house, hand-in-hand, and interviewed her.

She was in the bow-window, reading a translation of *The Deipnosophists* of Athenaeus.

"Good morning," she said, looking at her watch. "It is a little past our usual breakfast time, Margie, I think?"

"We have been looking for mushrooms, mother."

"Every investigation, says Athenaeus, which is guided by principles of Nature fixes its ultimate aim entirely on gratifying the stomach. Have you found any mushrooms?"

"Heaps, Mrs. Goodwin," said James.

"Mother," I said, "we want to tell you something."

"The fact is, Mrs. Goodwin——"

"We are engaged."

My mother liked James.

"Margie," she once said to me, "there is good in Mr. Cloyster. He is not for ever offering to pass me things." Time had not caused her to modify this opinion. She received our news calmly, and inquired into James's means and prospects. James had forty pounds and some odd silver. I had nothing.

The key-note of my mother's contribution to our conference was, "Wait."

"You are both young," she said.

She then kissed me, smiled contemplatively at James, and resumed her book.

When we were alone, "My darling," said James, "we must wait. Tomorrow I catch the boat for Weymouth. I shall go straight to London. My first manuscript shall be in an editor's hands on Wednesday morning. I will go, but I will come back."

I put my arms round his neck.

"My love," I said, "I trust you. Go. Always remember that I know you will succeed."

I kissed him.

"And when you have succeeded, come back."

Chapter 3

A HARMLESS DECEPTION

(Miss Margaret Goodwin's narrative continued)

They say that everyone is capable of one novel. And, in my opinion, most people could write one play.

Whether I wrote mine in an inspiration of despair, I cannot say. I wrote it.

Three years had passed, and James was still haggling with those who buy men's brains. His earnings were enough just to keep his head above water, but not enough to make us two one.

Perhaps, because everything is clear and easy for us now, I am gradually losing a proper appreciation of his struggle. That should never be. He did not win. But he did not lose; which means nearly as much. For it is almost less difficult to win than not to lose, so my mother has told me, in modern journalistic London. And I know that he would have won. The fact that he continued the fight as he did was in itself a pledge of ultimate victory. What he went through while trying with his pen to make a living for himself and me I learned from his letters.

"London," he wrote, "is not paved with gold; but in literary fields there are nuggets to be had by the light-

est scratching. And those nuggets are plays. A successful play gives you money and a name automatically.
What the ordinary writer makes in a year the successful dramatist receives, without labour, in a fortnight."
He went on to deplore his total lack of dramatic intuition. "Some men," he said, "have some of the qualifi-
cations while falling short of the others. They have a
sense of situation without the necessary tricks of tech-
nique. Or they sacrifice plot to atmosphere, or atmosphere to plot. I, worse luck, have not one single quali-
fication. The nursing of a climax, the tremendous
omissions in the dialogue, the knack of stage characterisation—all these things are, in some inexplicable way,
outside me."

It was this letter that set me thinking. Ever since
James had left the island, I had been chafing at the
helplessness of my position. While he toiled in London,
what was I doing? Nothing. I suppose I helped him in
a way. The thought of me would be with him always,
spurring him on to work, that the time of our separa-
tion might be less. But it was not enough. I wanted to
be *doing* something. . . . And it was during these
restless weeks that I wrote my play.

I think nothing will ever erase from my mind the
moment when the central idea of *The Girl who Waited*
came to me. It was a boisterous October evening. The
wind had been rising all day. Now the branches of the
lilac were dancing in the rush of the storm, and far out
in the bay one could see the white crests of the waves
gleaming through the growing darkness. We had just
finished tea. The lamp was lit in our little drawing-
room, and on the sofa, so placed that the light fell over
her left shoulder in the manner recommended by ocu-
lists, sat my mother with Schopenhauer's *Art of Literature*. Ponto slept on the rug.

Something in the unruffled peace of the scene tore

at my nerves. I have seldom felt so restless. It may have been the storm that made me so. I think myself that it was James's letter. The boat had been late that morning, owing to the weather, and I had not received the letter till after lunch. I listened to the howl of the wind, and longed to be out in it.

My mother looked at me over her book.

"You are restless, Margie," she said. "There is a volume of Marcus Aurelius on the table beside you, if you care to read."

"No, thank you, mother," I said. "I think I shall go for a walk."

"Wrap up well, my dear," she replied.

She then resumed her book.

I went out of our little garden, and stood on the cliff. The wind flew at me like some wild thing. Spray stung my face. I was filled with a wild exhilaration.

And then the idea came to me. The simplest, most dramatic idea. Quaint, whimsical, with just that suggestion of pathos blended with it which makes the fortunes of a play. The central idea, to be brief, of *The Girl who Waited*.

Of my Maenad tramp along the cliff-top with my brain afire, and my return, draggled and dripping, an hour late for dinner; of my writing and re-writing, of my tears and black depression, of the pens I wore out and the quires of paper I spoiled, and finally of the ecstasy of the day when the piece began to move and the characters to live, I need not speak. Anyone who has ever written will know the sensations. James must have gone through a hundred times what I went through once. At last, at long last, the play was finished.

For two days I gloated alone over the great pile of manuscript.

Then I went to my mother.

My diffidence was exquisite. It was all I could do to

tell her the nature of my request, when I spoke to her after lunch. At last she understood that I had written a play, and wished to read it to her. She took me to the bow-window with gentle solicitude, and waited for me to proceed.

At first she encouraged me, for I faltered over my opening words. But as I warmed to my work, and as my embarrassment left me, she no longer spoke. Her eyes were fixed intently upon the blue space beyond the lilac.

I read on and on, till at length my voice trailed over the last line, rose gallantly at the last fence, the single word *Curtain,* and abruptly broke. The strain had been too much for me.

Tenderly my mother drew me to the sofa; and quietly, with closed eyelids, I lay there until, in the soft cool of the evening, I asked for her verdict.

Seeing, as she did instantly, that it would be more dangerous to deny my request than to accede to it, she spoke.

"That there is an absence, my dear Margie, of any relationship with life, that not a single character is in any degree human, that passion and virtue and vice and real feeling are wanting—this surprises me more than I can tell you. I had expected to listen to a natural, ordinary, unactable episode arranged more or less in steichomuthics. There is no work so scholarly and engaging as the amateur's. But in your play I am amazed to find the touch of the professional and experienced playwright. Yes, my dear, you have proved that you happen to possess the quality—one that is most difficult to acquire—of surrounding a situation which is improbable enough to be convincing with that absurdly mechanical conversation which the theatre-going public demands. As your mother, I am disappointed. I had hoped for originality. As your literary well-wisher, I stifle my maternal feelings and congratulate you unreservedly."

I thanked my mother effusively. I think I cried a little.

She said affectionately that the hour had been one of great interest to her, and she added that she would be glad to be consulted with regard to the steps I contemplated taking in my literary future.

She then resumed her book.

I went to my room and re-read the last letter I had had from James.

The Barrel Club,
Covent Garden,
London.

MY DARLING MARGIE,—I am writing this line simply and solely for the selfish pleasure I gain from the act of writing to you. I know everything will come right some time or other, but at present I am suffering from a bad attack of the blues. I am like a general who has planned out a brilliant attack, and realises that he must fail for want of sufficient troops to carry a position, on the taking of which the whole success of the assault depends. Briefly, my position is like this. My name is pretty well known in a small sort of way among editors and the like as that of a man who can turn out fairly good stuff. Besides this, I have many influential friends. You see where this brings me? I am in the middle of my attacking movement, and I have not been beaten back; but the key to the enemy's position is still uncaptured. You know what this key is from my other letters. It's the stage. Ah, Margie, one acting play! Only one! It would mean everything. Apart from the actual triumph and the direct profits, it would bring so much with it. The enemy's flank would be turned, and the rest of the battle would become a mere rout. I should have an ac-

cepted position in the literary world which would
convert all the other avenues to wealth on which I
have my eye instantly into royal roads. Obstacles
would vanish. The fact that I was a successful playwright would make the acceptance of the sort of
work I am doing now inevitable, and I should get
paid ten times as well for it. And it would mean—
well, you know what it would mean, don't you?
Darling Margie, tell me again that I have your love,
that the waiting is not too hard, that you believe in
me. Dearest, it will come right in the end. Nothing
can prevent that. Love and the will of a man have
always beaten Time and Fate. Write to me, dear.

Ever your devoted
James.

How utterly free from thought of self! His magnificent loyalty forgot the dreadful tension of his own
great battle, and pictured only the tedium of waiting
which it was my part to endure.

I finished my letter to James very late that night. It
was a very long and explanatory letter, and it enclosed
my play.

The main point I aimed at was not to damp his
spirits. He would, I knew well, see that the play was
suitable for staging. He would, in short, see that I, an
inexperienced girl, had done what he, a trained professional writer, had failed to do. Lest, therefore, his
pique should kill admiration and pleasure when he
received my work, I wrote as one begging a favour.
"Here," I said, "we have the means to achieve all we
want. Do not—oh, do not—criticise. I have written
down the words. But the conception is yours. The play
was inspired by you. But for you I should never have
begun it. Take my play, James; take it as your own. For
yours it is. Put your name to it, and produce it, if you
love me, under your own signature. If this hurts your

pride, I will word my request differently. You alone are able to manage the business side of the production. You know the right men to go to. To approach them on behalf of a stranger's work is far less likely to lead to success. I have assumed, you will see, that the play is certain to be produced. But that will only be so if you adopt it as your own. Claim the authorship, and all will be well."

Much more I wrote to James in the same strain; and my reward came next day in the shape of a telegram: "Accept thankfully.—Cloyster."

Of the play and its reception by the public there is no need to speak. The criticisms were all favourable.

Neither the praise of the critics nor the applause of the public aroused any trace of jealousy in James. Their unanimous note of praise has been a source of pride to him. He is proud—ah, joy!—that I am to be his wife.

I have blotted the last page of this commonplace love-story of mine.

The moon has come out from behind a cloud, and the whole bay is one vast sheet of silver. I could sit here at my bedroom window and look at it all night. But then I should be sure to oversleep myself and be late for breakfast. I shall read what I have written once more, and then I shall go to bed.

I think I shall wear my white muslin tomorrow.

(End of Miss Margaret Goodwin's narrative.)

Part Two

James Orlebar Cloyster's Narrative

Chapter 1

THE INVASION OF BOHEMIA

It is curious to reflect that my marriage (which takes place today week) destroys once and for all my life's ambition. I have never won through to the goal I longed for, and now I never shall.

Ever since I can remember I have yearned to be known as a Bohemian. That was my ambition. I have ceased to struggle now. Married Bohemians live in Oakley Street, King's Road, Chelsea. We are to rent a house in Halkett Place.

Three years have passed since the excellent, but unsteady, steamship *Ibex* brought me from Guernsey to Southampton. It was a sleepy, hot, and sticky wreck that answered to the name of James Orlebar Cloyster that morning; but I had my first youth and forty pounds, so that soap and water, followed by coffee and an omelette, soon restored me.

The journey to Waterloo gave me opportunity for tobacco and reflection.

What chiefly exercised me, I remember, was the problem whether it was possible to be a Bohemian, and at the same time to be in love. Bohemia I looked on as a region where one became inevitably entangled with

women of unquestionable charm, but doubtful moral-
ity. There were supper parties. . . . Festive gatherings
in the old studio. . . . Babette. . . . Lucille. . . . The
artists' ball. . . . Were these things possible for a man
with an honest, earnest, whole-hearted affection?

The problem engaged me tensely till my ticket was
collected at Vauxhall. Just there the solution came. I
would be a Bohemian, but a misogynist. People would
say, "Dear old Jimmy Cloyster. How he hates women!"
It would add to my character a pleasant touch of dignity and reserve which would rather accentuate my
otherwise irresponsible way of living.

Little did the good Bohemians of the metropolis
know how keen a recruit the boat train was bringing to
them.

As a *pied-à-terre* I selected a cheap and dingy hotel in
York Street, and from this base I determined to locate
my proper sphere.

Chelsea was the first place that occurred to me.
There was St. John's Wood, of course, but that was
such a long way off. Chelsea was comparatively near to
the heart of things, and I had heard that one might
find there artistic people whose hand-to-mouth, Sat-
urnalian existence was redolent of that exquisite gaiety
which so attracted my own casual temperament.

Sallying out next morning into the brilliant sunshine
and the dusty rattle of York Street, I felt a sense of ela-
tion at the thought that the time for action had come. I
was in London. London! The home of the fragrant
motor-omnibus and the night-blooming Hooligan.
London, the battlefield of the literary aspirant since
Caxton invented the printing press. It seemed to me,
as I walked firmly across Westminster Bridge, that
Margie gazed at me with the lovelight in her eyes, and

that a species of amorous telepathy from Guernsey was girding me for the fight.

Manresa Road I had once heard mentioned as being the heart of Bohemian Chelsea. To Manresa Road, accordingly, I went, by way of St. James's Park, Buckingham Palace Road, and Lower Sloane Street. Thence to Sloane Square. Here I paused, for I knew that I had reached the last outpost of respectable, inartistic London.

"How sudden," I soliloquised, "is the change. Here I am in Sloane Square, regular, business-like, and unimaginative; while, a few hundred yards away, King's Road leads me into the very midst of genius, starvation, and possibly Free Love."

Sloane Square, indeed, gave me the impression, not so much of a suburb as of the suburban portion of a great London railway terminus. It was positively pretty. People were shopping with comparative leisure, omnibus horses were being rubbed down and watered on the west side of the Square, out of the way of the main stream of traffic. A postman, clearing the letter-box at the office, stopped his work momentarily to read the contents of a postcard. For the moment I understood Cæsar's feelings on the brink of the Rubicon, and the emotions of Cortes "when with eagle eyes he stared at the Pacific." I was on the threshold of great events. Behind me was orthodox London; before me the unknown.

It was distinctly a Cæsarian glance, full of deliberate revolt, that I bestowed upon the street called Sloane; that clean, orderly thoroughfare which leads to Knightsbridge, and thence either to the respectabilities of Kensington or the plush of Piccadilly.

Setting my hat at a wild angle, I stepped with a touch of *abandon* along the King's Road to meet the charming, impoverished artists whom our country refuses to recognise.

My first glimpse of the Manresa Road was, I confess, a complete disappointment. Never was Bohemianism more handicapped by its setting than that of Chelsea, if the Manresa Road was to be taken as a criterion. Along the uninviting uniformity of this street no trace of unorthodoxy was to be seen. There came no merry, roystering laughter from attic windows. No talented figures of idle geniuses fetched pints of beer from the public-house at the corner. No one dressed in an ancient ulster and a battered straw hat and puffing enormous clouds of blue smoke from a treasured clay pipe gazed philosophically into space from a doorway. In point of fact, save for a most conventional butcher-boy, I was alone in the street.

Then the explanation flashed upon me. I had been seen approaching. The word had been passed round. A stranger! The clique resents intrusion. It lies hid. These gay fellows see me all the time, and are secretly amused. But they do not know with whom they have to deal. I have come to join them, and join them I will. I am not easily beaten. I will outlast them. The joke shall be eventually against them, at some eccentric supper. I shall chaff them about how they tried to elude me, and failed.

The hours passed. Still no Bohemians. I began to grow hungry. I sprang on to a passing 'bus. It took me to Victoria. I lunched at the Shakespeare Hotel, smoked a pipe, and went out into the sunlight again. It had occurred to me that night was perhaps the best time for trapping my shy quarry. Possibly the revels did not begin in Manresa Road till darkness had fallen. I spent the afternoon and evening in the Park, dined at Lyons' Popular Café (it must be remembered that I was not yet a Bohemian, and consequently owed no deference to the traditions of the order); and returned at nine o'clock to the Manresa Road. Once more I drew blank. A barrel-organ played cake-walk airs in the middle of the road, but it played to an invisible audience. No bearded men danced can-cans around it, shouting merry jests to one another. Solitude reigned.

I wait. The duel continues. What grim determination, what perseverance can these Bohemians put into a mad jest! I find myself thinking how much better it would be were they to apply to their Art the same earnestness and fixity of purpose which they squander on a practical joke.

Evening fell. Blinds began to be drawn down. Lamps were lit behind them, one by one. Despair was gnawing at my heart, but still I waited.

Then, just as I was about to retire defeated, I was arrested by the appearance of a house numbered 93A.

At the first-floor window sat a man. He was writing. I could see his profile, his long untidy hair. I understood in a moment. This was no ordinary writer. He was one of those Bohemians whose wit had been exercised upon me so successfully. He was a literary man, and though he enjoyed the sport as much as any of the others he was under the absolute necessity of writing his copy up to time. Unobserved by his gay comrades, he had slipped away to his work. They were still watching me; but he, probably owing to a contract with some journal, was obliged to give up his share in their merriment and toil with his pen.

His pen fascinated me. I leaned against the railings of the house opposite, enthralled. Ever and anon he seemed to be consulting one or other of the books of reference piled up on each side of him. Doubtless he was preparing a scholarly column for a daily paper.

Presently a printer's devil would arrive, clamouring for his "copy." I knew exactly the sort of thing that happened. I had read about it in novels.

How unerring is instinct, if properly cultivated. Hardly had the clocks struck twelve when the emissaries—there were two of them, which showed the importance of their errand—walked briskly to No. 93A, and knocked at the door.

The writer heard the knock. He rose hurriedly, and began to collect his papers. Meanwhile, the knocking had been answered from within by the shooting of bolts, noises that were followed by the apparition of a female head.

A few brief questions and the emissaries entered. A pause.

The litterateur is warning the menials that their charge is sacred; that the sheets he has produced are impossible to replace. High words. Abrupt re-opening of the front door. Struggling humanity projected on to the pavement. Three persons—my scribe in the middle, an emissary on either side—stagger strangely past me. The scribe enters the purple night only under the stony compulsion of the emissaries.

What does this mean?

I have it. The emissaries have become over-anxious. They dare not face the responsibility of conveying the priceless copy to Fleet Street. They have completely lost their nerve. They insist upon the author accompanying them to see with his own eyes that all is well. They do not wish Posterity to hand their names down to eternal infamy as "the men who lost Blank's manuscript."

So, greatly against his will, he is dragged off.

My vigil is rewarded. No. 93A harbours a Bohemian. Let it be inhabited also by me.

I stepped across, and rang the bell.

The answer was a piercing scream.

"Ah, ha!" I said to myself complacently, "there are more Bohemians than one, then, in this house."

The female head again appeared.

"Not another? Oh, sir, say there ain't another wanted," said the head in a passionate Cockney accent.

"That is precisely what there is," I replied. "I want——"

"What for?"

"For something moderate."

"Well, that's a comfort in a wiy. Which of 'em is it you want? The first-floor back?"

"I have no doubt the first-floor back would do quite well."

My words had a curious effect. She scrutinised me suspiciously.

"Ho!" she said, with a sniff; "you don't seem to care much which it is you get."

"I don't," I said, "not particularly."

"Look 'ere," she exclaimed, "you jest 'op it. See? I don't want none of your 'arf-larks here, and, what's more, I won't 'ave 'em. I don't believe you're a copper at all."

"I'm not. Far from it."

"Then what d'yer mean coming 'ere saying you want my first-floor back?"

"But I do. Or any other room, if that is occupied."

" 'Ow! *Room?* Why didn't yer siy so? You'll pawdon me, sir, if I've said anything 'asty-like. I thought—but my mistake."

"Not at all. Can you let me have a room? I notice that the gentleman whom I have just seen——"

She cut me short. I was about to explain that I was a Bohemian, too.

" 'E's gorn for a stroll, sir. I expec' him back every moment. 'E's forgot 'is latchkey. Thet's why I'm sitting

up for 'im. Mrs. Driver my name is, sir. That's my
name, and well known in the neighbour'ood."

Mrs. Driver spoke earnestly, but breathlessly.

"I do not contemplate asking you, Mrs. Driver, to
give me the apartments already engaged by the literary
gentleman——"

"Yes, sir," she interpolated, "that's wot 'e wos, I mean
is. A literary gent."

"But have you not another room vacant?"

"The second-floor back, sir. Very comfortable, nice
room, sir. Shady in the morning, and gets the setting
sun."

Had the meteorological conditions been adverse to
the point of malignancy, I should have closed with her
terms. Simple agreements were ratified then and there
by the light of a candle in the passage, and I left the
house, promising to "come in" in the course of the following afternoon.

Chapter 2

I EVACUATE BOHEMIA

(James Orlebar Cloyster's narrative continued)

The three weeks which I spent at No. 93A mark an epoch in my life. It was during that period that I came nearest to realising my ambition to be a Bohemian; and at the end of the third week, for reasons which I shall state, I deserted Bohemia, firmly and with no longing, lingering glance behind, and settled down to the prosaic task of grubbing earnestly for money.

The second-floor back had a cupboard of a bedroom leading out of it. Even I, desirous as I was of seeing romance in everything, could not call my lodgings anything but dingy, dark, and commonplace. They were just like a million other of London's mean lodgings. The window looked out over a sea of backyards, bounded by tall, depressing houses, and intersected by clothes-lines. A cats' club (social, musical, and pugilistic) used to meet on the wall to the right of my window. One or two dissipated trees gave the finishing touch of gloom to the scene. Nor was the interior of the room more cheerful. The furniture had been put in during the reign of George III, and last dusted in that of William and Mary. A black horse-hair sofa ran along one wall. There was a deal table, a chair, and a rickety bookcase. It was a room for a realist to write in; and my style, such as it was, was bright and optimistic.

Once in, I set about the task of ornamenting my abode with much vigour. I had my own ideas of mural decoration. I papered the walls with editorial rejection forms, of which I was beginning to have a representative collection. Properly arranged, these look very striking. There is a good deal of variety about them. The ones I liked best were those which I received, at the rate of three a week, bearing a very pleasing picture, in green, of the publishing offices at the top of the sheet of note-paper. Scattered about in sufficient quantities, these lend an air of distinction to a room. *Pearson*'s *Magazine* also supplies a taking line in rejection forms. *Punch*'s I never cared for very much. Neat, I grant you; but, to my mind, too cold. I like a touch of colour in a rejection form.

In addition to these, I purchased from the grocer at the corner a collection of pictorial advertisements. What I had really wanted was the theatrical poster, printed and signed by well-known artists. But the grocer didn't keep them, and I was impatient to create my proper atmosphere. My next step was to buy a corncob pipe and a quantity of rank, jet-black tobacco. I hated both, and kept them more as ornaments than for use.

Then, having hacked my table about with a knife and battered it with a poker till it might have been the table of a shaggy and unrecognised genius, I settled down to work.

I was not a brilliant success. I had that "little knowledge" which is held to be such a dangerous thing. I had not plunged into the literary profession without learning a few facts about it. I had read nearly every journalistic novel and "Hints on Writing for the Papers" book that had ever been published. In theory I knew all that there was to be known about writing. Now, all my authorities were very strong on one point. "Write," they said, very loud and clear, "not what *you* like, but what editors like." I smiled to myself when I started. I felt that I had stolen a march on my rivals. "All round me," I said to myself, "are young authors bombarding editors with essays on Lucretius, translations of Martial, and disquisitions on Ionic comedy. I know too much for that. I work on a different plan." "Study the papers, and see what they want," said my authorities. I studied the papers. Some wanted one thing, apparently, others another. There was one group of three papers whose needs seemed to coincide, and I could see an article rejected by one paper being taken by another. This offered me a number of chances instead of one. I could back my MSS. to win or for a place. I began a serious siege of these three papers.

By the end of the second week I had had "Curious Freaks of Eccentric Testators," "Singular Scenes in Court," "Actors Who Have Died on the Stage," "Curious Scenes in Church," and seven others rejected by all three. Somehow this sort of writing is not so easy as it looks. A man who was on the staff of a weekly once told me that he had had two thousand of these articles printed since he started—poor devil. He had the knack. I could never get it. I sent up fifty-three in all in the first year of my literary life, and only two stuck. I got fifteen shillings from one periodical for "Men Who Have Missed Their Own Weddings," and, later, a guinea from the same for "Single Day Marriages." That paper has a penchant for the love-interest. Yet when I sent it my "Duchesses Who Have Married Dustmen," it came back by the early post next day. That was to me the worst part of those grey days. I had my victories, but they were always followed by a series of defeats. I would have a manuscript accepted by an editor. "Hullo," I would say, "here's the man at last, the Editor-Who-Believes-In-Me. Let the thing go on." I would send him off another manuscript. He would take it. Victory, by Jove! Then—*wonk!* Back would come my third effort with the curtest of refusals. I always imagined editors in those days to be pettish, whimsical men who amused themselves by taking up a beginner, and then, wearying of the sport, dropped him back into the slime from which they had picked him.

In the intervals of articles I wrote short stories, again for the same three papers. As before, I studied these papers carefully to see what they wanted; then worked out a mechanical plot, invariably with a quarrel in the first part, an accident, and a rescue in the middle, and a reconciliation at the end—told it in a style that makes me hot all over when I think of it, and sent it up, enclosing a stamped addressed envelope in case of rejection. A very useful precaution, as it always turned out.

It was the little knowledge to which I have referred above which kept my walls so thickly covered with rejection forms. I was in precisely the same condition as a man who has been taught the rudiments of boxing. I knew just enough to hamper me, and not enough to do me any good. If I had simply blundered straight at my work and written just what occurred to me in my own style, I should have done much better. I have a sense of humour. I deliberately stifled it. For it I substituted a grisly kind of playfulness. My hero called my heroine "little woman," and the concluding passage where he kissed her was written in a sly, roguish vein, for which I suppose I shall have to atone in the next world. Only the editor of the *Colney Hatch Argus* could have accepted work like mine. Yet I toiled on.

It was about the middle of my third week at No. 93A that I definitely decided to throw over my authorities, and work by the light of my own intelligence.

Nearly all my authorities had been very severe on the practice of verse-writing. It was, they asserted, what all young beginners tried to do, and it was the one thing editors would never look at. In the first ardour of my revolt I determined to do a set of verses.

It happened that the weather had been very bad for the last few days. After a month and a half of sunshine the rain had suddenly begun to fall. I took this as my topic. It was raining at the time. I wrote a satirical poem, full of quaint rhymes.

I had always had rather a turn for serious verse. It struck me that the rain might be treated poetically as well as satirically. That night I sent off two sets of verses to a daily and an evening paper. Next day both were in print, with my initials to them.

I began to see light.

"Verse is the thing," I said. "I will reorganise my campaign. First the skirmishers, then the real attack. I will peg along with verses till somebody begins to take my stories and articles."

I felt easier in my mind than I had felt for some time. A story came back by the nine o'clock post from a monthly magazine (to which I had sent it from mere bravado), but the thing did not depress me. I got out my glue-pot and began to fasten the rejection form to the wall, whistling a lively air as I did so.

While I was engaged in this occupation there was a testy rap at the door, and Mrs. Driver appeared. She eyed my manœuvres with the rejection form with a severe frown. After a preliminary sniff she embarked upon a rapid lecture on what she called my irregular and untidy habits. I had turned her second-floor back, she declared, into a pig-stye.

"Sech a litter," she said.

"But," I protested, "this is a Bohemian house, is it not?"

She appeared so shocked—indeed, so infuriated, that I dared not give her time to answer.

"The gentleman below, he's not very tidy," I added diplomatically.

"Wot gent below?" said Mrs. Driver.

I reminded her of the night of my arrival.

"Oh, *'im,*" she said, shaken. "Well, 'e's not come back."

"Mrs. Driver," I said sternly, "you said he'd gone out for a stroll. I refuse to believe that any man would stroll for three weeks."

"So I did say it," was the defiant reply. "I said it so as you shouldn't be put off coming. You looked a steady young feller, and I wanted a let. Wish I'd told you the truth, if it 'ad a-stopped you."

"What is the truth?"

" 'E was a wrong 'un, 'e wos. Writing begging letters to parties as was a bit soft, that wos *'is* little gime. But 'e wos a bit too clever one day, and the coppers got 'im. Now you know!"

Mrs. Driver paused after this outburst, and allowed her eye to wander slowly and ominously round my walls.

I was deeply moved. My one link with Bohemia had turned out a fraud.

Mrs. Driver's voice roused me from my meditations.

"I must arst you to be good enough, if *you* please, kindly to remove those there bits of paper."

She pointed to the rejection forms.

I hesitated. I felt that it was a thing that ought to be broken gently.

"The fact is, Mrs. Driver," I said, "and no one can

regret it more deeply than I do—the fact is, they're stuck on with glue."

Two minutes later I had received my marching orders, and the room was still echoing with the slam of the door as it closed behind the indignant form of my landlady.

Chapter 3

THE *ORB*

(James Orlebar Cloyster's narrative continued)

The problem of lodgings in London is an easy one to a man with an adequate supply of money in his pocket. The only difficulty is to select the most suitable, to single out from the eager crowd the ideal landlady.

Evicted from No. 93A, it seemed to me that I had better abandon Bohemia; postpone my connection with that land of lotus-eaters for the moment, while I provided myself with the means of paying rent and buying dinners. Farther down the King's Road there were comfortable rooms to be had for a moderate sum per week. They were prosaic, but inexpensive. I chose Walpole Street. A fairly large bed-sitting room was vacant at No. 23. I took it, and settled down seriously to make my writing pay.

There were advantages in Walpole Street which Manresa Road had lacked. For one thing, there was more air, and it smelt less than the Manresa Road air. Walpole Street is bounded by Burton Court, where the Household Brigade plays cricket, and the breezes from the river come to it without much interruption. There was also more quiet. No. 23 is the last house in the street, and, even when I sat with my window open, the noise of traffic from the King's Road was faint and rather pleasant. It was an excellent spot for a man who meant to work. Except for a certain difficulty in getting my landlady and her daughters out of the room when they came to clear away my meals and talk about the better days they had seen, and a few imbroglios with the eight cats which infested the house, it was the best spot, I think, that I could have chosen.

Living a life ruled by the strictest economy, I gradually forged ahead. Verse, light and serious, continued my long suit. I generally managed to place two of each brand a week; and that meant two guineas, sometimes more. One particularly pleasing thing about this verse-writing was that there was no delay, as there was with my prose. I would write a set of verses for a daily paper after tea, walk to Fleet Street with them at half-past six, thus getting a little exercise; leave them at the office; and I would see them in print in the next morning's issue. Payment was equally prompt. The rule was, Send in your bill before five on Wednesday, and call for payment on Friday at seven. Thus I had always enough money to keep me going during the week.

In addition to verses, I kept turning out a great quantity of prose, fiction, and otherwise, but without much success. The visits of the postmen were the big events of the day at that time. Before I had been in Walpole Street a week I could tell by ear the difference between a rejected manuscript and an ordinary letter. There is a certain solid *plop* about the fall of the former which not even a long envelope full of proofs can imitate successfully.

I worked extraordinarily hard at that time. All day, sometimes. The thought of Margie waiting in Guernsey kept me writing when I should have done better to have taken a rest. My earnings were small in proportion to my labour. The guineas I made, except from

verse, were like the ounce of gold to the ton of ore. I
no longer papered the walls with rejection forms; but
this was from choice, not from necessity. I had plenty
of material, had I cared to use it.

I made a little money, of course. My takings for the
first month amounted to £9 10s. I notched double figures in the next with £11 1s. 6d. Then I dropped to £7
0s. 6d. It was not starvation, but it was still more unlike
matrimony.

But at the end of the sixth month there happened to
me what, looking back, I consider to be the greatest
piece of good fortune of my life. I received a literary
introduction. Some authorities scoff at literary in-
troductions. They say that editors read everything,
whether they know the author or not. So they do; and,
if the work is not good, a letter to the editor from a
man who once met his cousin at a garden-party is not
likely to induce him to print it. There is no journalistic
"ring" in the sense in which the word is generally used;
but there are undoubtedly a certain number of men
who know the ropes, and can act as pilots in a strange
sea; and an introduction brings one into touch with
them. There is a world of difference between contributing blindly work which seems suitable to the style
of a paper and sending in matter designed to attract
the editor personally.

Mr. Macrae, whose pupil I had been at Cambridge,
was the author of my letter of introduction. At St. Gabriel's, Mr. Macrae had been a man for whom I enter-
tained awe and respect. Likes and dislikes in connection with one's tutor seemed outside the question. Only
a chance episode had shown me that my tutor was a
mortal with a mortal's limitations. We were bicycling
together one day along the Trumpington Road, when
a form appeared, coming to meet us. My tutor's
speech grew more and more halting as the form came

nearer. At last he stopped talking altogether, and wob-
bled in his saddle. The man bowed to him, and, as if he
had won through some fiery ordeal, he shot ahead like
a gay professional rider. When I drew level with him,
he said, "That, Mr. Cloyster, is my tailor."

Mr. Macrae was typical of the University don who is
Scotch. He had married the senior historian of Newn-
ham. He lived (and still lives) by proxy. His publishers
order his existence. His honeymoon had been placed at
the disposal of these gentlemen, and they had allotted
to that period an edition of Aristotle's Ethics. Aristotle,
accordingly, received the most scholarly attention from
the recently united couple somewhere on the slopes of
Mount Parnassus. All the reviews were satisfactory.

In my third year at St. Gabriel's it was popularly supposed that Master Pericles Æschylus, Mr. Macrae's
infant son, was turned to correct my Latin prose,
though my Iambics were withheld from him at the
request of the family doctor.

The letter which Pericles Æschylus's father had addressed to me was one of the pleasantest surprises I
have ever had. It ran as follows:

> *St. Gabriel's College,*
> *Cambridge.*
>
> MY DEAR CLOYSTER,—The divergence of our
> duties and pleasures during your residence here
> caused us to see but little of each other. Would it
> had been otherwise! And too often our intercourse
> had—on my side—a distinctly professional flavour.
> Your attitude towards your religious obligations
> was, I fear, something to seek. Indeed, the line,
> *"Pastor deorum cultor et infrequens,"* might have been
> directly inspired by your views on the keeping of
> Chapels. On the other hand, your contributions to
> our musical festivities had the true Aristophanes
> *panache.*

I hear you are devoting yourself to literature, and I beg that you will avail yourself of the enclosed note, which is addressed to a personal friend of mine.

Believe me,

Your well-wisher,
David Ossian Macrae.

The enclosure bore this inscription:

CHARLES FERMIN, ESQ.,
Offices of the *Orb,*
Strand,
London.

I had received the letter at breakfast. I took a cab, and drove straight to the *Orb.*

A painted hand, marked "Editorial," indicated a flight of stairs. At the top of these I was confronted by a glass door, beyond which, entrenched behind a desk, sat a cynical-looking youth. A smaller boy in the background talked into a telephone. Both were giggling. On seeing me the slightly larger of the two advanced with a half-hearted attempt at solemnity, though unable to resist a Parthian shaft at his companion, who was seized on the instant with a paroxysm of suppressed hysteria.

My letter was taken down a mysterious stone passage. After some waiting the messenger returned with the request that I would come back at eleven, as Mr. Fermin would be very busy till then.

I went out into the Strand, and sought a neighbouring hostelry. It was essential that I should be brilliant at the coming interview, if only spirituously brilliant; and I wished to remove a sensation of stomachic emptiness, such as I had been wont to feel at school when approaching the headmaster's study.

At eleven I returned, and asked again for Mr. Fermin; and presently he appeared—a tall, thin man, who
gave one the impression of being in a hurry. I knew
him by reputation as a famous quarter-miler. He had
been president of the O.U.A.C. some years back. He
looked as if at any moment he might dash off in any
direction at quarter-mile pace.

We shook hands, and I tried to look intelligent.

"Sorry to have to keep you waiting," he said, as we
walked to his club; "but we are always rather busy between ten and eleven, putting the column through.
Gresham and I do 'On Your Way,' you know. The last
copy has to be down by half-past ten."

We arrived at the Club, and sat in a corner of the
lower smoking-room.

"Macrae says that you are going in for writing. Of
course, I'll do anything I can, but it isn't easy to help a
man. As it happens, though, I can put you in the way
of something, if it's your style of work. Do you ever do
verse?"

I felt like a batsman who sees a slow full-toss sailing
through the air.

"It's the only thing I can get taken," I said. "I've had
quite a lot in the *Chronicle* and occasional bits in other
papers."

He seemed relieved.

"Oh, that's all right, then," he said. "You know 'On
Your Way.' Perhaps you'd care to come in and do that
for a bit? It's only holiday work, but it'll last five weeks.
And if you do it all right I can get you the whole of the
holiday work on the column. That comes to a good lot
in the year. We're always taking odd days off. Can you
come up at a moment's notice?"

"Easily," I said.

"Then, you see, if you did that you would drop into
the next vacancy on the column. There's no saying

when one may occur. It's like the General Election. It may happen tomorrow, or not for years. Still, you'd be on the spot in case."

"It's awfully good of you."

"Not at all. As a matter of fact, I was rather in difficulties about getting a holiday man. I'm off to Scotland the day after tomorrow, and I had to find a sub. Well, then, will you come in on Monday?"

"All right."

"You've had no experience of newspaper work, have you?"

"No."

"Well, all the work at the *Orb's* done between nine and eleven. You must be there at nine sharp. Literally sharp, I mean. Not half-past. And you'd better do some stuff overnight for the first week or so. You'll find working in the office difficult till you get used to it. Of course, though, you'll always have Gresham there, so there's no need to get worried. He can fill the column himself, if he's pushed. Four or five really good paragraphs a day and an occasional set of verses are all he'll want from you."

"I see."

"On Monday, then. Nine sharp. Good-bye."

I walked home along Piccadilly with almost a cake-walk stride. At last I was in the inner circle.

An *Orb* cart passed me. I nodded cheerfully to the driver. He was one of *Us*.

Chapter 4

JULIAN EVERSLEIGH

(James Orlebar Cloyster's narrative continued)

I determined to celebrate the occasion by dining out, going to a theatre, and having supper afterwards, none of which things were ordinarily within my means. I had not been to a theatre since I had arrived in town; and, except on Saturday nights, I always cooked my own dinner, a process which was cheap, and which appealed to the passion for Bohemianism which I had not wholly cast out of me.

The morning paper informed me that there were eleven musical comedies, three Shakespeare plays, a blank verse drama, and two comedies ("last weeks") for me to choose from. I bought a stall at the Briggs Theatre. Stanley Briggs, who afterwards came to bulk large in my small world, was playing there in a musical comedy which had had even more than the customary musical-comedy success.

London by night had always had an immense fascination for me. Coming out of the restaurant after supper, I felt no inclination to return to my lodgings, and end the greatest night of my life tamely with a book and a pipe. Here was I, a young man, fortified by an excellent supper, in the heart of Stevenson's London.

Why should I have no New Arabian Night adventure?
I would stroll about for half an hour, and give London
a chance of living up to its reputation.

I walked slowly along Piccadilly, and turned up Rupert Street. A magic name. Prince Florizel of Bohemia
had ended his days there in his tobacconist's divan. Mr.
Gilbert's Policeman Forth had been discovered there
by the men of London at the end of his long wander-
ings through Soho. Probably, if the truth were known,
Rudolf Rassendyl had spent part of his time there. It
could not be that Rupert Street would send me empty
away.

My confidence was not abused. Turning into Rupert
Court, a dark and suggestive passage some short distance up the street on the right, I found a curious little
comedy being played.

A door gave on to the deserted passageway, and on
each side of it stood a man—the lurcher type of man
that is bred of London streets. The door opened in-
wards. Another man stepped out. The hands of one of
the lurchers flew to the newcomer's mouth. The hands
of the other lurcher flew to the newcomer's pockets.

At that moment I advanced.

The lurchers vanished noiselessly and instanta-
neously.

Their victim held out his hand.

"Come in, won't you?" he said, smiling sleepily at me.

I followed him in, murmuring something about
"caught in the act."

He repeated the phrase as we went upstairs.

" 'Caught in the act.' Yes, they are ingenious crea-
tures. Let me introduce myself. My name is Julian
Eversleigh. Sit down, won't you? Excuse me for a moment."

He crossed to a writing-table.

Julian Eversleigh inhabited a single room of irregular shape. It was small, and situated immediately under the roof. One side had a window which overlooked Rupert Court. The view from it was, however, restricted, because the window was inset, so that the walls projecting on either side prevented one seeing more than a yard or two of the court.

The room contained a hammock, a large tin bath, propped up against the wall, a big wardrobe, a couple of bookcases, a deal writing-table—at which the proprietor was now sitting with a pen in his mouth, gazing at the ceiling—and a divan-like formation of rugs and cube sugar boxes.

The owner of this mixed lot of furniture wore a very faded blue serge suit, the trousers baggy at the knees and the coat threadbare at the elbows. He had the odd expression which green eyes combined with red hair give a man.

"Caught in the act," he was murmuring. "Caught in the act."

The phrase seemed to fascinate him.

I had established myself on the divan, and was puffing at a cigar, which I had bought by way of setting the coping-stone on my night's extravagance, before he got up from his writing.

"Those fellows," he said, producing a bottle of whisky and a syphon from one of the lower drawers of the wardrobe, "did me a double service. They introduced me to you—say when—and they gave me——"

"When."

"——an idea."

"But how did it happen?" I asked.

"Quite simple," he answered. "You see, my friends, when they call on me late at night, can't get in by knocking at the front door. It is a shop-door, and is locked early. Vancott, my landlord, is a baker, and, as he has to be up making muffins somewhere about five in the morning—we all have our troubles—he does not stop up late. So people who want me go into the court, and see whether my lamp is burning by the window. If it is, they stand below and shout, 'Julian,' till I open the door into the court. That's what happened tonight. I heard my name called, went down, and walked into the arms of the enterprising gentlemen whom you chanced to notice. They must have been very hungry, for even if they had carried the job through they could not have expected to make their fortunes. In point of fact, they would have cleared one-and-threepence. But when you're hungry you can see no further than the pit of your stomach. Do you know, I almost sympathise with the poor brutes. People sometimes say to me, 'What are you?' I have often half a mind to reply, 'I have been hungry.' My stars, be hungry once, and you're educated, if you don't die of it, for a lifetime."

This sort of talk from a stranger might have been the prelude to an appeal for financial assistance.

He dissipated that half-born thought.

"Don't be uneasy," he said; "you have not been lured up here by the ruse of a clever borrower. I can do a bit of touching when in the mood, mind you, but you're safe. You are here because I see that you are a pleasant fellow."

"Thank you," I said.

"Besides," he continued, "I am not hungry at present. In fact, I shall never be hungry again."

"You're lucky," I remarked.

"I am. I am the fortunate possessor of the knack of writing advertisements."

"Indeed," I said, feeling awkward, for I saw that I ought to be impressed.

"Ah!" he said, laughing outright. "You're not impressed in the least, really. But I'll ask you to consider what advertisements mean. First, they are the life-essence of every newspaper, every periodical, and every book."

"Every book?"

"Practically, yes. Most books contain some latent support of a fashion in clothes or food or drink, or of some pleasant spot or phase of benevolence or vice, all of which form the interest of one or other of the sections of society, which sections require publicity at all costs for their respective interests."

I was about to probe searchingly into so optimistic a view of modern authorship, but he stalled me off by proceeding rapidly with his discourse.

"Apart, however, from the less obvious modes of advertising, you'll agree that this is the age of all ages for the man who can write puffs. 'Good wine needs no bush' has become a trade paradox, 'Judge by appearances,' a commercial platitude. The man who is ambitious and industrious turns his trick of writing into purely literary channels, and becomes a novelist. The man who is not ambitious and not industrious, and who does not relish the prospect of becoming a loafer in Strand wine-shops, writes advertisements. The gold-bearing area is always growing. It's a Tom Tiddler's ground. It is simply a question of picking up the gold and silver. The industrious man picks up as much as he wants. Personally, I am easily content. An occasional nugget satisfies me. Here's tonight's nugget, for instance."

I took the paper he handed to me. It bore the words:

Caught in the Act

Caught in the Act of drinking Skeffington's Sloe Gin, a man will always present a happy and smiling appearance. Skeffington's Sloe Gin adds a crowning pleasure to prosperity, and is a consolation in adversity. Of all Grocers.

"Skeffington's," he said, "pay me well. I'm worth money to them, and they know it. At present they are giving me a retainer to keep my work exclusively for them. The stuff they have put on the market is neither better nor worse than the average sloe gin. But my advertisements have given it a tremendous vogue. It is the only brand that grocers stock. Since I made the firm issue a weekly paper called *Skeffington's Poultry Farmer,* free to all country customers, the consumption of sloe gin has been enormous among agriculturists. My idea, too, of supplying suburban buyers gratis with a small drawing-book, skeleton illustrations, and four coloured chalks, has made the drink popular with children. You must have seen the poster I designed. There's a reduced copy behind you. The father of a family is unwrapping a bottle of Skeffington's Sloe Gin. His little ones crowd round him, laughing and clapping their hands. The man's wife is seen peeping roguishly in through the door. Beneath is the popular catch-phrase, "Ain't mother going to 'ave none?"

"You're a genius," I cried.

"Hardly that," he said. "At least, I have no infinite capacity for taking pains. I am one of Nature's slackers. Despite my talent for drawing up advertisements, I am often in great straits owing to my natural inertia and a passionate love of sleep. I sleep on the slightest provocation or excuse. I will back myself to sleep against any-one in the world, no age, weight, or colour barred. You, I should say, are of a different temperament. More energetic. The Get On or Get Out sort of thing. The Young Hustler."

"Rather," I replied briskly, "I am in love."

"So am I," said Julian Eversleigh. "Hopelessly, how-ever. Give us a match."

After that we confirmed our friendship by smoking a number of pipes together.

Chapter 5

THE COLUMN

(James Orlebar Cloyster's narrative continued)

After the first week "On Your Way," on the *Orb*, offered hardly any difficulty. The source of material was the morning papers, which were placed in a pile on our table at nine o'clock. The halfpenny papers were our principal support. Gresham and I each took one, and picked it clean. We attended first to the Subject of the Day. This was generally good for two or three paragraphs of verbal fooling. There was a sort of tradition that the first half-dozen paragraphs should be topical. The rest might be topical or not, as occasion served.

The column usually opened with a one-line pun—Gresham's invention.

Gresham was a man of unparalleled energy and ingenuity. He had created several of the typical characters who appeared from time to time in "On Your Way," as, for instance, Mrs. Jenkinson, our Mrs. Malaprop, and Jones junior, our "howler" manufacturing schoolboy. He was also a stout apostle of a mode of expression which he called "funny language." Thus, instead of writing boldly: "There is a rumour that——," I was taught to say, "It has got about that——." This sounds

funnier in print, so Gresham said. I could never see it
myself.

Gresham had a way of seizing on any bizarre incident reported in the morning papers, enfolding it in
"funny language," adding a pun, and thus making it
his own. He had a cunning mastery of periphrasis, and
a telling command of adverbs.

Here is an illustration. An account was given one
morning by the Central news of the breaking into of a
house at Johnsonville (Mich.) by a negro, who had
stolen a quantity of greenbacks. The thief, escaping
across some fields, was attacked by a cow, which, after
severely injuring the negro, ate the greenbacks.

Gresham's unacknowledged version of the episode
ran as follows:—

"The sleepy god had got the stranglehold on John
Denville when Cæsar Bones, a coloured gentleman,
entered John's house at Johnsonville (Mich.) about
midnight. Did the nocturnal caller disturb his slumber-
ing host? No. Cæsar Bones has the finer feelings. But
as he was noiselessly retiring, what did he see? Why, a
pile of greenbacks which John had thoughtlessly put
away in a fire-proof safe."

To prevent the story being cut out by the editor, who
revised all the proofs of the column, with the words
"too long" scribbled against it, Gresham continued his
tale in another paragraph.

" 'Dis am berry insecure,' murmured the visitor to
himself, transplanting the notes in a neighbourly way
into his pocket. Mark the sequel. The noble Cæsar
met, on his homeward path, an irritable cudster. The
encounter was brief. Cæsar went weak in the second
round, and took the count in the third. Elated by her
triumph, and hungry from her exertions, the horned
quadruped nosed the wad of paper money and dar-
ingly devoured it. Cæsar has told the court that if he is

convicted of felony, he will arraign the owner of the os-
trich-like bovine on a charge of receiving stolen goods.
The owner merely ejaculates 'Black male!' "

On his day Gresham could write the column and
have a hundred lines over by ten o'clock. I, too, found
plenty of copy as a rule, though I continued my practice of doing a few paragraphs overnight. But every
now and then fearful days would come, when the
papers were empty of material for our purposes, and
when two out of every half-dozen paragraphs which we
did succeed in hammering out were returned deleted
on the editor's proof.

The tension at these times used to be acute. The
head printer would send up a relay of small and
grubby boys to remind us that "On Your Way" was
fifty lines short. At ten o'clock he would come in person, and be plaintive.

Gresham, the old hand, applied to such occasions
desperate remedies. He would manufacture out of
even the most pointless item of news two paragraphs
by adding to his first the words, "This reminds us of
Mr. Punch's famous story." He would then go through
the bound volumes of *Punch*—we had about a dozen in
the room—with lightning speed until he chanced upon
a more or less appropriate tag.

Those were mornings when verses would be padded
out from three stanzas to five, Gresham turning them
out under fifteen minutes. He had a wonderful facility
for verse.

As a last expedient one fell back upon a standing column, a moth-eaten collection of alleged jests which had
been set up years ago to meet the worst emergencies. It
was, however, considered a confession of weakness and
a degradation to use this column.

We had also in our drawer a book of American witticisms, published in New York. To cut one out, pref-

ace it with "A good American story comes to hand," and pin it on a slip was a pleasing variation of the usual mode of constructing a paragraph. Gresham and I each had our favourite method. Personally, I had always a partiality for dealing with "buffers." "The brakes refused to act, and the train struck the buffers at the end of the platform" invariably suggested that if elderly gentlemen would abstain from loitering on railway platforms, they would not get hurt in this way.

Gresham had a similar liking for "turns." "The performance at the Frivoli Music Hall was in full swing when the scenery was noticed to be on fire. The audience got a turn. An extra turn."

Julian Eversleigh, to whom I told my experiences on the *Orb,* said he admired the spirit with which I entered into my duties. He said, moreover, that I had a future before me, not only as a journalist, but as a writer.

Nor, indeed, could I help seeing for myself that I was getting on. I was making a fair income now, and had every prospect of making a much better one. My market was not restricted. Verses, articles, and fiction from my pen were being accepted with moderate regularity by many of the minor periodicals. My scope was growing distinctly wider. I found, too, that my work seemed to meet with a good deal more success when I sent it in from the *Orb,* with a letter to the editor on *Orb* notepaper.

Altogether, my five weeks on the *Orb* were invaluable to me. I ought to have paid rather than have taken payment for working on the column. By the time Fermin came back from Scotland to turn me out, I was a professional. I had learned the art of writing against time. I had learned to ignore noise, which, for a writer in London, is the most valuable quality of all. Every day at the *Orb* I had had to turn out my stuff with the

hum of the Strand traffic in my ears, varied by an occasional barrel-organ, the whistling of popular songs
by the printers, whose window faced ours, and the clatter of a typewriter in the next room. Often I had to
turn out a paragraph or a verse while listening and
making appropriate replies to some other member of
the staff, who had wandered into our room to pass the
time of day or read out a bit of his own stuff which had
happened to please him particularly. All this gave me a
power of concentration, without which writing is difficult in this city of noises.

The friendship I formed with Gresham too, besides
being pleasant, was of infinite service to me. He knew
all about the game. I followed his advice, and pros-
pered. His encouragement was as valuable as his advice. He was my pilot, and saw me, at great trouble to
himself, through the dangerous waters.

I foresaw that the future held out positive hope that
my marriage with Margaret would become possible.
And yet——

Pausing in the midst of my castle-building, I suffered
a sense of revulsion. I had been brought up to believe
that the only adjective that could be coupled with the
noun "journalism" was "precarious." Was I not, as Gresham would have said, solving an addition sum in in-
fantile poultry before their mother, the feathered deni-
zen of the farmyard, had lured them from their shell?
Was I not mistaking a flash in the pan for a genuine
success?

These thoughts numbed my fingers in the act of
writing to Margaret.

Instead, therefore, of the jubilant letter I had intended to send her, I wrote one of quite a different
tone. I mentioned the arduous nature of my work. I
referred to the struggle in which I was engaged. I indicated cleverly that I was a man of extraordinary

courage battling with fate. I implied that I made just
enough to live on.

It would have been cruel to arouse expectations
which might never be fulfilled. In this letter, accordingly, and in subsequent letters, I rather went to the
opposite extreme. Out of pure regard for Margaret, I
painted my case unnecessarily black. Considerations of
a similar nature prompted me to keep on my lodging
in Walpole Street. I had two rooms instead of one, but
they were furnished severely and with nothing but the
barest necessaries.

I told myself through it all that I loved Margaret as
dearly as ever. Yet there were moments, and they
seemed to come more frequently as the days went on,
when I found myself wondering. Did I really want to
give up all this? The untidiness, the scratch meals, the
nights with Julian? And, when I was honest, I answered, No.

Somehow Margaret seemed out of place in this new
world of mine.

Chapter 6

NEW YEAR'S EVE

(James Orlebar Cloyster's narrative continued)

The morning of New Year's Eve was a memorable one for me. My first novel was accepted. Not an ambitious volume. It was rather short, and the plot was not obtrusive. The sporting gentlemen who accepted it, however—Messrs. Prodder and Way—seemed pleased with it; though, when I suggested a sum in cash in advance of royalties, they displayed a most embarrassing coyness—and also, as events turned out, good sense.

I carried the good news to Julian, whom I found, as usual, asleep in his hammock. I had fallen into the habit of calling on him after my *Orb* work. He was generally sleepy when I arrived, at half-past eleven, and while we talked I used to make his breakfast act as a sort of early lunch for myself. He said that the people of the house had begun by trying to make the arrival of his breakfast coincide with the completion of his toilet; that this had proved so irksome that they had struck; and that finally it had been agreed on both sides that the meal should be put in his room at eleven o'clock, whether he was dressed or not. He said that he often saw his breakfast come in, and would drowsily determine to consume it hot. But he had never had the

59

energy to do so. Once, indeed, he had mistaken the time, and had confidently expected that the morning of a hot breakfast had come at last. He was dressed by nine, and had sat for two hours gloating over the prospect of steaming coffee and frizzling bacon. On that particular morning, however, there had been some domestic tragedy—the firing of a chimney or the illness of a cook—and at eleven o'clock, not breakfast, but an apology for its absence had been brought to him. This embittered Julian. He gave up the unequal contest, and he has frequently confessed to me that cold breakfast is an acquired, yet not unpleasant, taste.

He woke up when I came in, and, after hearing my news and congratulating me, began to open the letters that lay on the table at his side.

One of the envelopes had Skeffington's trade mark stamped upon it, and contained a bank-note and a sheet closely type-written on both sides.

"Half a second, Jimmy," said he, and began to read.

I poured myself out a cup of cold coffee, and, avoiding the bacon and eggs, which lay embalmed in frozen grease, began to lunch off bread and marmalade.

"I'll do it," he burst out when he had finished. "It's a sweat—a fearful sweat, but——

"Skeffington's have written urging me to undertake a rather original advertising scheme. They're very pressing, and they've enclosed a tenner in advance. They want me to do them a tragedy in four acts. I sent them the scenario last week. I sketched out a skeleton plot in which the hero is addicted to a strictly moderate use of Skeffington's Sloe Gin. His wife adopts every conceivable measure to wean him from this harmless, even praiseworthy indulgence. At the end of the second act she thinks she has cured him. He has promised to gratify what he regards as merely a capricious whim on her part. 'I will give—yes, I will give it up, darling!'

'George! George!' She falls on his neck. Over her shoulder he winks at the audience, who realise that there is more to come. Curtain. In Act 3 the husband is seen sitting alone in his study. His wife has gone to a party. The man searches in a cupboard for something to read. Instead of a novel, however, he lights on a bottle of Skeffington's Sloe Gin. Instantly the old overwhelming craving returns. He hesitates. What does it matter? She will never know. He gulps down glass after glass. He sinks into an intoxicated stupor. His wife enters. Curtain again. Act 4. The draught of nectar tasted in the former act after a period of enforced abstinence has produced a deadly reaction. The husband, who previously improved his health, his temper, and his intellect by a strictly moderate use of Skeffington's Sloe Gin, has now become a ghastly dipsomaniac. His wife, realising too late the awful effect of her idiotic antagonism to Skeffington's, experiences the keenest pangs of despair. She drinks laudanum, and the tragedy is complete."

"Fine," I said, finishing the coffee.

"In a deferential postscript," said Julian, "Skeffington's suggest an alternative ending, that the wife should drink, not laudanum, but Sloe Gin, and grow, under its benign influence, resigned to the fate she has brought on her husband and herself. Resignation gives way to hope. She devotes her life to the care of the inebriate man, and, by way of pathetic retribution, she lives precisely long enough to nurse him back to sanity. Which finale do you prefer?"

"Yours!" I said.

"Thank you," said Julian, considerably gratified. "So do I. It's terser, more dramatic, and altogether a better advertisement. Skeffington's make jolly good sloe gin, but they can't arouse pity and terror. Yes, I'll do it; but first let me spend the tenner."

"I'm taking a holiday, too, today," I said. "How can we amuse ourselves?"

Julian had opened the last of his letters. He held up two cards.

"Tickets for Covent Garden Ball tonight," he said. "Why not come? It's sure to be a good one."

"I should like to," I said. "Thanks."

Julian dropped from his hammock, and began to get his bath ready.

We arranged to dine early at the Maison Suisse in Rupert Street—*table d'hôte* one franc, plus twopence for mad'moiselle—and go on to the gallery of a first night. I was to dress for Covent Garden at Julian's after the theatre, because white waistcoats and the franc *table d'hôte* didn't go well together.

When I dined out, I usually went to the Maison Suisse. I shall never have the chance of going again, even if, as a married man, I were allowed to do so, for it has been pulled down to make room for the Hicks Theatre in Shaftesbury Avenue. When I did not dine there, I attended a quaint survival of last century's coffee-houses in Glasshouse Street: Tall, pew-like boxes, wooden tables without table-cloths, panelled walls; an excellent menu of chops, steaks, fried eggs, sausages, and other British products. Once the resort of bucks and Macaronis, Ford's coffee-house I found frequented by a strange assortment of individuals, some of whom resembled bookmakers' touts, others clerks of an inexplicably rustic type. Who these people really were I never discovered.

"I generally have supper at Pepolo's," said Julian, as we left the theatre, "before a Covent Garden Ball. Shall we go on there?"

There are two entrances to Pepolo's restaurant, one leading to the ground floor, the other to the brasserie in the basement. I liked to spend an hour or so there occasionally, smoking and watching the crowd. Every sixth visit on an average I would happen upon some-body interesting among the ordinary throng of medical students and third-rate clerks—watery-eyed old fellows who remembered Cremorne, a mahogany derelict who had spent his youth on the sea when liners were sail-ing-ships, and the apprentices, terrorised by bullying mates and the rollers of the Bay, lay howling in the scuppers and prayed to be thrown overboard. He told me of one voyage on which the Malay cook went mad, and, escaping into the ratlines, shot down a dozen of the crew before he himself was sniped.

The supper tables are separated from the brasserie by a line of stucco arches, and as it was now a quarter to twelve the place was full. At a first glance it seemed that there were no empty supper tables. Presently, however, we saw one, laid for four, at which only one man was sitting.

"Hullo!" said Julian, "there's Malim. Let's go and see if we can push into his table. Well, Malim, how are you? Do you know Cloyster?"

Mr. Malim had a lofty expression. I should have put him down as a scholarly recluse. His first words upset this view somewhat.

"Coming to Covent Garden?" he said, genially. "I am. So is Kit. She'll be down soon."

"Good," said Julian; "may Jimmy and I have supper at your table?"

"Do," said Malim. "Plenty of room. We'd better order our food and not wait for her."

We took our places, and looked round us. The hum of conversation was persistent. It rose above the clatter of the supper tables and the sudden bursts of laughter.

It was now five minutes to twelve. All at once those nearest the door sprang to their feet. A girl in scarlet and black had come in.

"Ah, there's Kit at last," said Malim.

"They're cheering her," said Julian.

As he spoke, the tentative murmur of a cheer was caught up by everyone. Men leaped upon chairs and tables.

"Hullo, hullo, hullo!" said Kit, reaching us. "Kiddie, when they do that it makes me feel shy."

She was laughing like a child. She leaned across the table, put her arms round Malim's neck, and kissed him. She glanced at us.

Malim smiled quietly, but said nothing.

She kissed Julian, and she kissed me.

"Now we're all friends," she said, sitting down.

"Better know each other's names," said Malim. "Kit, this is Mr. Cloyster. Mr. Cloyster, may I introduce you to my wife?"

Chapter 7

I MEET MR. THOMAS BLAKE

(James Orlebar Cloyster's narrative continued)

Someone had told me that the glory of Covent Garden Ball had departed. It may be so. Yet the floor, with its strange conglomeration of music-hall artists, callow university men, shady horse-dealers, and raucous military infants, had an atmosphere of more than meretricious gaiety. The close of an old year and the birth of a new one touch the toughest.

The band was working away with a strident brassiness which filled the room with noise. The women's dresses were a shriek of colour. The vulgarity of the scene was so immense as to be almost admirable. It was certainly interesting.

Watching his opportunity, Julian presently drew me aside into the smoking-room.

"Malim," he said, "has paid you a great compliment."

"Really," I said, rather surprised, for Julian's acquaintance had done nothing more, to my knowledge, than give me a cigar and a whiskey-and-soda.

"He's introduced you to his wife."

"Very good of him, I'm sure."

"You don't understand. You see Kit for what she is: a pretty, good-natured creature bred in the gutter. But

65

Malim—well, he's in the Foreign Office and is secretary to Sir George Grant."

"Then what in Heaven's name," I cried, "induced him to marry——"

"My dear Jimmy," said Julian, adroitly avoiding the arm of an exuberant lady impersonating Winter, and making fair practice with her detachable icicles, "it was Kit or no one. Just consider Malim's position, which was that of thousands of other men of his type. They are the cleverest men of their schools; they are the intellectual stars of their 'Varsities. I was at Oxford with Malim. He was a sort of tin god. Double-first and all that. Just like all the rest of them. They get what is looked upon as a splendid appointment under Government. They come to London, hire comfortable chambers or a flat, go off to their office in the morning, leave it in the evening, and are given a salary which increases by regular gradations from an initial two hundred a year. Say that a man begins this kind of work at twenty-four. What are his matrimonial prospects? His office work occupies his entire attention (the idea that Government clerks don't work is a fiction preserved merely for the writers of burlesque) from the moment he wakes in the morning until dinner. His leisure extends, roughly speaking, from eight-thirty until twelve. The man whom I am discussing, and of whom Malim is a type, is, as I have already proved, intellectual. He has, therefore, ambitions. The more intellectual he is the more he loathes the stupid routine of his daily task. Thus his leisure is his most valuable possession. There are books he wants to read—those which he liked in the days previous to his slavery—and new ones which he sees published every day. There are plays he wants to see performed. And there are subjects on which he would like to write—would give his left hand to write, if the loss of that limb wouldn't dis-

qualify him for his post. Where is his social chance? It
surely exists only in the utter abandonment of his personal projects. And to go out when one is tied to the
clock is a poor sort of game. But suppose he *does* seek
the society of what friends he can muster in London. Is
he made much of, fussed over? Not a bit of it.
Brainless subalterns, ridiculous mishipmen, have, in
the eyes of the girl whom he has come to see, a reputation that he can never win. They're in the Service;
they're so dashing; they're so charmingly extravagant;
they're so tremendous in face of an emergency that
their conversational limitations of "Yes" and "No" are
hailed as brilliant flights of genius. Their inane anec-
dotes, their pointless observations are positively
courted. It is they who retire to the conservatory with
the divine Violet, whose face is like the Venus of Milo's,
whose hair (one hears) reaches to her knees, whose
eyes are like blue saucers, and whose complexion is a
pink poem. It is Jane, the stumpy, the flat-footed—
Jane, who wears glasses and has all the virtues which
are supposed to go with indigestion: big hands and an
enormous waist—Jane, I repeat, who is told off to talk
to a man like Malim. If, on the other hand, he and his
fellows refuse to put on evening clothes and be bored
to death of an evening, who can blame them? If they
deliberately find enough satisfaction for their needs in
the company of a circle of men friends and the casual
pleasures of the town, selfishness is the last epithet with
which their behaviour can be charged. Unselfishness
has been their curse. No sane person would, of his own
accord, become the automaton that a Government office requires. Pressure on the part of relations, of
parents, has been brought to bear on them. The steady
employment, the graduated income, the pension—that
fatal pension—has been danced by their fathers and
their mothers and their Uncle Johns before their eyes.

Appeals have been made to them on filial, not to say religious, grounds. Threats would have availed nothing; but appeals—downright tearful appeals from mamma, husky, hand-gripping appeals from papa— that is what has made escape impossible. A huge act of unselfishness has been compelled; a lifetime of reactionary egotism is inevitable and legitimate. I was wrong when I said Malim was typical. He has to the good an ingenuity which assists naturally in the solution of the problem of self and circumstance. A year or two ago chance brought him in contact with Kit. They struck up a friendship. He became an habitué at the Fried Fish Shop in Tottenham Court Road. Whenever we questioned his taste he said that a physician recommended fish as a tonic for the brain. But it was not his brain that took Malim to the fried fish shop. It was his heart. He loved Kit, and presently he married her. One would have said this was an impossible step. Misery for Malim's people, his friends, himself, and afterwards for Kit. But Nature has endowed both Malim and Kit with extraordinary commonsense. He kept to his flat; she kept to her job in the fried fish shop. Only, instead of living in, she was able to retire after her day's work to a little house which he hired for her in the Hampstead Road. Her work, for which she is eminently fitted, keeps her out of mischief. His flat gives the impression to his family and the head of his department that he is still a bachelor. Thus, all goes well."

"I've often read in the police reports," I said, "of persons who lead double lives, and I'm much interested in——"

Malim and Kit bore down upon us. We rose.

"It's the march past," observed the former. "Come upstairs."

"Kiddie," said Kit, "give me your arm."

At half-past four we were in Wellington Street. It

was a fine, mild morning, and in the queer light of the false dawn we betook ourselves to the Old Hummums for breakfast. Other couples had done the same. The steps of the Hummums facing the market harboured already a waiting crowd. The doors were to be opened at five. We also found places on the stone steps. The market was alive with porters, who hailed our appearance with every profession of delight. Early hours would seem to lend a certain acidity to their badinage. By-and-by a more personal note crept into their facetious comments. Two guardsmen on the top step suddenly displayed, in return, a very creditable gift of repartee. Covent Garden market was delighted. It felt the stern joy which warriors feel with foemen worthy of their steel. It suspended its juggling feats with vegetable baskets, and devoted itself exclusively to the task of silencing our guns. Porters, costers, and the riff-raff of the streets crowded in a semicircle around us. Just then it was borne in on us how small our number was. A solid phalanx of the toughest customers in London faced us. Behind this semicircle a line of carts had been drawn up. Unseen enemies from behind this laager now began to amuse themselves by bombarding us with the product of the market garden. Tomatoes, cauliflowers, and potatoes came hurtling into our midst. I saw Julian consulting his watch. "Five minutes more," he said. I had noticed some minutes back that the ardour of the attack seemed to centre round one man in particular—a short, very burly man in a costume that seemed somehow vaguely nautical. His face wore the expression of one cheerfully conscious of being well on the road to intoxication. He was the ringleader. It was he who threw the largest cabbage, the most *passé* tomato. I don't suppose he had ever enjoyed himself so much in his life. He was standing now on a cart full of potatoes, and firing them in with tremendous force.

Kit saw him too.

"Why, there's that blackguard Tom!" she cried.

She had been told to sit down behind Malim for safety. Before anyone could stop her, or had guessed her intention, she had pushed her way through us and stepped out into the road.

It was so unexpected that there was an involuntary lull in the proceedings.

"Tom!"

She pointed an accusing finger at the man, who gaped beerily.

"Tom, who pinched farver's best trousers, and popped them?"

There was a roar of laughter. A moment before, and Tom had been the pet of the market, the energetic leader, the champion potato-slinger. Now he was a thing of derision. His friends took up the question. Keen anxiety was expressed on all sides as to the fate of father's trousers. He was requested to be a man and speak up.

The uproar died away as it was seen that Kit had not yet finished.

"Cheese it, some of yer," shouted a voice. "The lady wants to orsk him somefin' else."

"Tom," said Kit, "who was sent with tuppence to buy postage-stamps and spent it on beer?"

The question was well received by the audience. Tom was beaten. A potato, vast and nobbly, fell from his palsied hand. He was speechless. Then he began to stammer.

"Just you stop it, Tom," shouted Kit triumphantly. "Just you stop it, d'you 'ear, you stop it."

She turned towards us on the steps, and, taking us all into her confidence, added: " 'E's a nice thing to 'ave for a bruvver, anyway."

Then she rejoined Malim, amid peals of laughter from both armies. It was a Homeric incident.

Only a half-hearted attempt was made to renew the attack. And when the door of the Hummums at last opened, Malim observed to Julian and me, as we squashed our way in, that if a man's wife's relations were always as opportune as Kit's, the greatest objection to them would be removed.

Chapter 8

I MEET THE
REV. JOHN HATTON

(James Orlebar Cloyster's narrative continued)

I saw a great deal of Malim after that. He and Julian became my two chief mainstays when I felt in need of society. Malim was a man of delicate literary skill, a genuine lover of books, a severe critic of modern fiction. Our tastes were in the main identical, though it was always a blow to me that he could see nothing humorous in Mr. George Ade, whose Fables I knew nearly by heart. The more robust type of humour left him cold.

In all other respects we agreed.

There is a never-failing fascination in a man with a secret. It gave me a pleasant feeling of being behind the scenes, to watch Malim, sitting in his armchair, the essence of everything that was conventional and respectable, with Eton and Oxford written all over him, and to think that he was married all the while to an employee in a Tottenham Court Road fried-fish shop.

Kit never appeared in the flat; but Malim went nearly every evening to the little villa. Sometimes he took Julian and myself, more often myself alone, Julian being ever disinclined to move far from his hammock.

The more I saw of Kit the more thoroughly I realized how eminently fitted she was to be Malim's wife. It was a union of opposites. Except for the type of fiction provided by "penny libraries of powerful stories," Kit had probably not read more than half a dozen books in her life. Grimm's fairy stories she recollected dimly, and she betrayed a surprising acquaintance with at least three of Ouida's novels. I fancy that Malim appeared to her as a sort of combination of fairy prince and Ouida guardsman. He exhibited the Oxford manner at times rather noticeably. Kit loved it.

Till I saw them together I had thought Kit's accent and her incessant mangling of the King's English would have jarred upon Malim. But I soon found that I was wrong. He did not appear to notice.

I learned from Kit, in the course of my first visit to the villa, some further particulars respecting her brother Tom, the potato-thrower of Covent Garden Market. Mr. Thomas Blake, it seemed, was the proprietor and skipper of a barge. A pleasant enough fellow when sober, but too much given to what Kit described as "his drop." He had apparently left home under something of a cloud, though whether this had anything to do with "father's trousers" I never knew. Kit said she had not seen him for some years, though each had known the other's address. It seemed that the Blake family were not great correspondents.

"Have you ever met John Hatton?" asked Malim one night after dinner at his flat.

"John Hatton?" I answered. "No. Who is he?"

"A parson. A very good fellow. You ought to know him. He's a man with a number of widely different interests. We were at Trinity together. He jumps from one thing to another, but he's frightfully keen about whatever he does. Someone was saying that he was running a boys' club in the thickest part of Lambeth."

"There might be copy in it," I said.

"Or ideas for advertisements for Julian," said Malim. "Anyway, I'll introduce you to him. Have you ever been in the Barrel?"

"What's the Barrel?"

"The Barrel is a club. It gets the name from the fact that it's the only club in England that allows, and indeed urges, its members to sit on a barrel. John Hatton is sometimes to be found there. Come round to it to-morrow night."

"All right," I replied. "Where is it?"

"A hundred and fifty-three, York Street, Covent Garden. First floor."

"Very well," I said. "I'll meet you there at twelve o'clock. I can't come sooner because I've got a story to write."

Twelve had just struck when I walked up York Street looking for No. 153.

The house was brilliantly lighted on the first floor. The street door opened on to a staircase, and as I mounted it the sound of a piano and a singing voice reached me. At the top of the stairs I caught sight of a waiter loaded with glasses. I called to him.

"Mr. Cloyster, sir? Yessir. I'll find out whether Mr. Malim can see you, sir."

Malim came out to me. "Hatton's not here," he said, "but come in. There's a smoking concert going on."

He took me into the room, the windows of which I had seen from the street.

There was a burst of cheering as we entered the room. The song was finished, and there was a movement among the audience. "It's the interval," said Malim.

Men surged out of the packed front room into the passage, and then into a sort of bar parlour. Malim and I also made our way there. "That's the fetish of the club," said Malim, pointing to a barrel standing on end; "and I'll introduce you to the man who is sitting on it. He's little Michael, the musical critic. They once put on an operetta of his at the Court. It ran about two nights, but he reckons all the events of the world from the date of its production."

"Mr. Cloyster—Mr. Michael."

The musician hopped down from the barrel and shook hands. He was a dapper little person, and had a trick of punctuating every sentence with a snigger.

"Cheer-o," he said genially. "Is this your first visit?"

I said it was.

"Then sit on the barrel. We are the only club in London who can offer you the privilege." Accordingly I sat on the barrel, and through a murmur of applause I could hear Michael telling someone that he'd first seen that barrel five years before his operetta came out at the Court.

At that moment a venerable figure strode with dignity into the bar.

"Maundrell," said Malim to me. "The last of the old Bohemians. An old actor. Always wears the steeple hat and a long coat with skirts."

The survivor of the days of Kean uttered a bellow for whisky-and-water. "That barrel," he said, "reminds me of Buckstone's days at the Haymarket. After the performance we used to meet at the Café de l'Europe, a few yards from the theatre. Our secret society sat there."

"What was the society called, Mr. Maundrell?" asked a new member with unusual intrepidity.

"Its name," replied the white-headed actor simply, "I shall not divulge. It was not, however, altogether unconnected with the Pink Men of the Blue Mountains. We used to sit, we who were initiated, in a circle. We met to discuss the business of the society. Oh, we were

the observed of all observers, I can assure you. Our society was extensive. It had its offshoots in foreign
lands. Well, we at these meetings used to sit round a
barrel—a great big barrel, which had a hole in the top.
The barrel was not merely an ornament, for through
the hole in the top we threw any scraps and odds and
ends we did not want. Bits of tobacco, bread, marrow
bones, the dregs of our glasses—anything and everything went into the barrel. And so it happened, as the
barrel became fuller and fuller, strange animals made
their appearance—animals of peculiar shape and form
crawled out of the barrel and would attempt to escape
across the floor. But we were on their tracks. We saw
them. We headed them off with our sticks, and we
chased them back again to the place where they had
been born and bred. We poked them in, sir, with our
sticks."

Mr. Maundrell emitted a placid chuckle at this
reminiscence.

"A good many members of this club," whispered
Malim to me, "would have gone back into that barrel."

A bell sounded. "That's for the second part to
begin," said Malim.

We herded back along the passage. A voice cried,
"Be seated, please, gentlemen."

At the far end of the room was a table for the chairman and the committee, and to the left stood a piano.
Everyone had now sat down except the chairman, who
was apparently not in the room. There was a pause.
Then a man from the audience whooped sharply and
clambered over the table and into the place of the
chairman. He tapped twice with the mallet. "Get out of
that chair," yelled various voices.

"Gentlemen," said the man in the chair. A howl of
execration went up, and simultaneously the door was
flung open. A double file of white-robed Druids came,
chanting, into the room.

The Druids carried in with them a small portable tree which they proceeded to set upright. The chant now became extremely topical. Each Druid sang a verse in turn, while his fellow Druids danced a stately measure round the tree. As the verse was being sung, an imitation granite altar was hastily erected.

The man in the chair, who had so far smoked a cigarette in silence, now tapped again with his mallet. "Gentlemen," he observed.

The Druids ended their song abruptly, and made a dash at the occupant of the chair. The audience stood up. "A victim for our ancient rites!" screamed the Druids, falling upon the man and dragging him towards the property altar.

The victim showed every sign of objection to early English rites; but he was dislodged, and after being dragged, struggling, across the table, subsided quickly on the floor. The mob surged about and around him. He was hidden from view. His position, however, could be located by a series of piercing shrieks.

The door again opened. Mr. Maundrell, the real chairman of the evening, stood on the threshold. "Chair!" was now the word that arose on every side, and at this signal the Druids disappeared at a trot past the long-bearded, impassive Mr. Maundrell. Their victim followed them, but before he did so he picked up his trousers which were lying on the carpet.

All the time this scene had been going on, I fancied I recognised the man in the chair. In a flash I remembered. It was Dawkins who had coached First Trinity, and whom I, as a visitor once at the crew's training dinner, had last seen going through the ancient and honourable process of de-bagging at the hands of his lighthearted boat.

"Come on," said Malim. "Godfrey Lane's going to sing a patriotic song. They *will* let him do it. We'll go down to the Temple and find John Hatton."

We left the Barrel at about one o'clock. It was a typical London late autumn night. Quiet with the peace of a humming top; warm with the heat generated from mellow asphalt and resinous wood-paving.

We turned from Bedford Street eastwards along the Strand.

Between one and two the Strand is as empty as it ever is. It is given over to lurchers and policemen. Fleet Street reproduces for this one hour the Sahara.

"When I knock at the Temple gate late at night," said Malim, "and am admitted by the night porter, I always feel a pleasantly archaic touch."

I agreed with him. The process seemed a quaint admixture of an Oxford or Cambridge college, Gottingen, and a feudal keep. And after the gate had been closed behind one, it was difficult to realise that within a few yards of an academic system of lawns and buildings full of living traditions and associations which wainscoting and winding stairs engender, lay the modern world, its American invaders, its new humour, its women's clubs, its long firms, its musical comedies, its Park Lane, and its Strand with the hub of the universe projecting from the roadway at Charing Cross, plain for Englishmen to gloat over and for foreigners to envy.

Sixty-two Harcourt Buildings is emblazoned with many names, including that of the Rev. John Hatton. The oak was not sported, and our rap at the inner door was immediately answered by a shout of "Come in!" As we opened it we heard a peculiar whirring sound. "Road skates," said Hatton, gracefully circling the table and then coming to a standstill. I was introduced. "I'm very glad to see you both," he said. "The two other men I share these rooms with have gone away, so I'm killing time by training for my road-skate tour abroad. It's trying for one's ankles."

"Could you go downstairs on them?" said Malim.

"Certainly," he replied, "I'll do so now. And when we're down, I'll have a little practice in the open."

Whereupon he skated to the landing, scrambled down the stairs, sped up Middle Temple Lane, and called the porter to let us out into Fleet Street. He struck me as a man who differed in some respects from the popular conception of a curate.

"I'll race you to Ludgate Circus and back," said the clergyman.

"You're too fast," said Malim; "it must be a handicap."

"We might do it level in a cab," said I, for I saw a hansom crawling towards us.

"Done," said the Rev. John Hatton. "Done, for half-a-crown!"

I climbed into the hansom, and Malim, about to follow me, found that a constable, to whom the soil of the City had given spontaneous birth, was standing at his shoulder. "Wot's the game?" inquired the officer, with tender solicitude.

"A fine night, Perkins," remarked Hatton.

"A fine morning, beggin' your pardon, sir," said the policeman facetiously. He seemed to be an acquaintance of the skater.

"Reliability trials," continued Hatton. "Be good enough to start us, Perkins."

"Very good, sir," said Perkins.

"Drive to Ludgate Circus and back, and beat the gentleman on the skates," said Malim to our driver, who was taking the race as though he assisted at such events in the course of his daily duty.

"Hi shall say, 'Are you ready? Horf!' "

"We shall have Perkins applying to the Jockey Club for Ernest Willoughby's job," whispered Malim.

"Are you ready? Horf!"

Hatton was first off the mark. He raced down the incline to the Circus at a tremendous speed. He was just in sight as he swung laboriously round and headed for home. But meeting him on our outward journey, we noticed that the upward slope was distressing him. "Shall we do it?" we asked.

"Yessir," said our driver. And now we, too, were on the up grade. We went up the hill at a gallop: were equal with Hatton at Fetter Lane, and reached the Temple Gate yards to the good.

The ancient driver of a four-wheeler had been the witness of the finish.

He gazed with displeasure upon us.

"This 'ere's a nice use ter put Fleet Street to, I don't think," he said coldly.

This sarcastic rebuke rather damped us, and after Hatton had paid Malim his half-crown, and had invited me to visit him, we departed.

"Queer chap, Hatton," said Malim as we walked up the Strand.

I was to discover at no distant date that he was distinctly a many-sided man. I have met a good many clergymen in my time, but I have never come across one quite like the Rev. John Hatton.

Chapter 9

JULIAN LEARNS MY SECRET

(James Orlebar Cloyster's narrative continued)

A difficulty in the life of a literary man in London is the question of getting systematic exercise. At school and college I had been accustomed to play games every day, and now I felt the change acutely.

It was through this that I first became really intimate with John Hatton, and incidentally with Sidney Price, of the Moon Assurance Company. I happened to mention my trouble one night in Hatton's rooms. I had been there frequently since my first visit.

"None of my waistcoats fit," I remarked.

"My dear fellow," said Hatton, "I'll give you exercise and to spare; that is to say, if you can box."

"I'm not a champion," I said; "but I'm fond of it. I shouldn't mind taking up boxing again. There's nothing like it for exercise."

"Quite right, James," he replied; "and exercise, as I often tell my boys, is essential."

"What boys?" I asked.

"My club boys," said Hatton. "They belong to the most dingy quarter of the whole of London—South Lambeth. They are not hooligans. They are not so interesting as that. They represent the class of youth that

81

is a stratum or two above hooliganism. Frightful weeds.
They lack the robust animalism of the class below
them, and they lack the intelligence of the class above
them. The fellows at my club are mostly hard-working
mechanics and under-paid office boys. They have
nothing approaching a sense of humour or the instinct
of sport."

"Not very encouraging," I said.

"Nor picturesque," said Hatton; "and that is why
they've been so neglected. There is romance in an out-
and-out hooligan. It interests people to reform him.
But to the outsider my boys are dull. I don't find them
so. But then I know them. Boxing lessons are just what
they want. In fact, I was telling Sidney Price, an insurance clerk who lives in Lambeth and helps me at the
club, only yesterday how much I wished we could teach
them to use the gloves."

"I'll take it on, then, Hatton, if you like," I said. "It
ought to keep me in form."

I found that it did. I ceased to be aware of my liver.
That winter I was able to work to good purpose, and
the result was that I arrived. It dawned upon me at last
that the "precarious" idea was played out. One could
see too plainly the white sheet and phosphorus.

And I was happy. Happier, perhaps, than I had ever
hoped to be. Happier, in a sense, than I can hope to be
again. I had congenial work, and, what is more, I had
congenial friends.

What friends they were!

Julian—I seem to see him now sprawling in his hammock, sucking his pipe, planning an advertisement, or
propounding some whimsical theory of life; and in his
eyes he bears the pain of one whose love and life are
spoilt. Julian—no longer my friend.

Kit and Malim—what evenings are suggested by
those names.

Evenings alone with Malim at his flat in Vernon Place. An unimpeachable dinner, a hand at picquet, midnight talk with the blue smoke wreathing round our heads.

Well, Malim and I are unlikely to meet again in Vernon Place. Nor shall we foregather at the little house in the Hampstead Road, the house which Kit enveloped in an inimitable air of domesticity. Her past had not been unconnected with the minor stage. She could play on the piano from ear, and sing the songs of the street with a charming cockney twang. But there was nothing of the stage about her now. She was born for domesticity and, as the wife of Malim, she wished to forget all that had gone before. She even hesitated to give us her wonderful imitations of the customers at the fried fish shop, because in her heart she did not think such impersonations altogether suitable for a respectable married woman.

It was Malim who got me elected to the Barrel Club. I take it that I shall pay few more visits there.

I have mentioned at this point the love of my old friends who made my first years in London a period of happiness, since it was in this month of April that I had a momentous conversation with Julian about Margaret.

He had come to Walpole Street to use my typewriter, and seemed amazed to find that I was still living in much the same style as I had always done.

"Let me see," he said. "How long is it since I was here last?"

"You came some time before Christmas."

"Ah, yes," he said reminiscently. "I was doing a lot of travelling just then." And he added, thoughtfully, "What a curious fellow you are, Jimmy. Here are you making——" He glanced at me.

"Oh, say a thousand a year."

"——Fifteen hundred a year, and you live in pre-

cisely the same shoddy surroundings as you did when
your manuscripts were responsible for an extra size in
waste-paper baskets. I was surprised to hear that you
were still in Walpole Street. I supposed that, at any
rate, you had taken the whole house."

His eyes raked the little sitting-room from the sham
marble mantelpiece to the bamboo cabinet. I surveyed
it, too, and suddenly it did seem unnecessarily
wretched and depressing.

Julian looked at me curiously.

"There's some mystery here," he said.

"Don't be an ass, Julian," I replied weakly.

"It's no good denying it," he retorted; "there's some
mystery. You're a materialist. You don't live like this
from choice. If you were to follow your own inclina-
tions, you'd do things in the best style you could run to.
You'd be in Jermyn Street; you'd have your man, a cottage in Surrey; you'd entertain, go out a good deal.
You'd certainly give up these dingy quarters. My
friendship for you deplores a mammoth skeleton in
your cupboard, James. My study of advertising tells me
that this paltry existence of yours does not adequately
push your name before the public. You're losing
money, you're——"

"Stop, Julian," I exclaimed.

"*Cherchez*," he continued, "*cherchez*——"

"Stop! Confound you, stop! I tell you——"

"Come," he said laughing. "I mustn't force your confidence; but I can't help feeling it's odd——"

"When I came to London," I said, firmly, "I was
most desperately in love. I was to make a fortune, incidentally my name, marry, and live happily ever after.
There seemed last year nothing complex about that
programme. It seemed almost too simple. I even, like a
fool, thought to add an extra touch of piquancy to it by
endeavouring to be a Bohemian. I then discovered that

what I was attempting was not so simple as I had imagined. To begin with, Bohemians diffuse their brains in every direction except that where bread-and-butter comes from. I found, too, that unless one earns bread-and-butter, one has to sprint very fast to the workhouse door to prevent oneself starving before one gets there; so I dropped Bohemia and I dropped many other pleasant fictions as well. I took to examining pavements, saw how hard they were, had a look at the gutters, and saw how broad they were. I noticed the accumulation of dirt on the house fronts, the actual proportions of industrial buildings. I observed closely the price of food, clothes, and roofs."

"You became a realist."

"Yes; I read a good deal of Gissing about then, and it scared me. I pitied myself. And after that came pity for the girl I loved. I swore that I would never let her come to my side in the ring where the monster Poverty and I were fighting. If you've been there you've been in hell. And if you come out with your soul alive you can't tell other people what it felt like. They couldn't understand."

Julian nodded. "I understand, you know," he said gravely.

"Yes, you've been there," I said. "Well, you've seen that my little turn-up with the monster was short and sharp. It wasn't one of the old-fashioned, forty-round, most-of-a-lifetime, feint-for-an-opening, in-and-out affairs. Our pace was too fast for that. We went at it both hands, fighting all the time. I was going for the knockout in the first round. Not your method, Julian."

"No," said Julian; "it's not my method. I treat the monster rather as a wild animal than as a hooligan; and hearing that wild animals won't do more than sniff at you if you lie perfectly still, I adopted that ruse towards him to save myself the trouble of a conflict.

But the effect of lying perfectly still was that I used to fall asleep; and that works satisfactorily."

"Julian," I said, "I detect a touch of envy in your voice. You try to keep it out, but you can't. Wait a bit, though. I haven't finished.

"As you know, I had the monster down in less than no time. I said to myself, 'I've won. I'll write to Margaret, and tell her so!' Do you know I had actually begun to write the letter when another thought struck me. One that started me sweating and shaking. 'The monster,' I said again to myself, 'the monster is devilish cunning. Perhaps he's only shamming! It looks as if he were beaten. Suppose it's only a feint to get me off my guard. Suppose he just wants me to take my eyes off him so that he may get at me again as soon as I've begun to look for a comfortable chair and a mantel-piece to rest my feet on!' I told myself that I wouldn't risk bringing Margaret over. I didn't dare chance her being with me if ever I had to go back into the ring. So I kept jumping and stamping on the monster. The referee had given me the fight and had gone away; and, with no one to stop me, I kicked the life out of him."

"No, you didn't," interrupted Julian. "Excuse me, I'm sure you didn't. I often wake up and hear him prowling about."

"Yes; but there's a separate monster set apart for each of us. It's Fate who arranges the programme, and, by stress of business, Fate postpones many contests so late that before they can take place the man has died. Those who die before their fight comes on are called rich men. To return, however, to my own monster: I was at last convinced that he was dead a thousand times——"

"How long have you had this conviction?" asked Julian.

"The absolute certainty that my monster has ceased

to exist came to me this morning whilst I brushed my hair."

"Ah," said Julian; "and now, I suppose, you really will write to Miss Margaret——" He paused.

"Goodwin?"

"To Miss Margaret Goodwin," he repeated.

"Look here, Julian," I said irritably; "it's no use your repeating every observation I make as though you were Massa Johnson on Margate Sands."

"What's the matter?"

I was silent for a moment. Then I confessed.

"Julian," I said, "I can't write to her. You need neither say that I'm a blackguard nor that you're sorry for us both. At this present moment I've no more affection for Margaret than I have for this chair. When precisely I left off caring for her I don't know. Why I ever thought I loved her I don't know, either. But ever since I came to London all the love I did have for her has been ebbing away every day."

"Had you met many people before you met her?" asked Julian slowly.

"No one that counted. Not a woman that counted, that's to say. I am shy with women. I can talk to them in a sort of way, but I never seem able to get intimate. Margaret was different. She saved my life, and we spent the summer in Guernsey together."

"And you seriously expected not to fall in love?" Julian laughed "My dear Jimmy, you ought to write a psychological novel."

"Possibly. But, in the meantime, what am I to do?"

Julian stood up.

"She's in love with you, I suppose?"

"Yes."

He stood looking at me.

"Well, can't you speak?" I said.

He turned away, shrugging his shoulders. "One's got

one's own right and one's own wrong," he grumbled, lighting his pipe.

"I know what you're thinking," I said.

He would not look at me.

"You're thinking," I went on, "what a cad I am not to have written that letter." I sat down resting my head on my hands. After all—love and liberty—they're both very sweet.

"I'm thinking," said Julian, watching the smoke from his pipe abstractedly, "that you will probably write tonight; and I think I know how you're feeling."

"Julian," I said, "must it be tonight? Why? The letter shall go. But must it be tonight?"

Julian hesitated.

"No," he said; "but you've made up your mind, so why put off the inevitable?"

"I can't," I exclaimed; "oh, I really can't. I must have my freedom a little longer."

"You must give it up some day. It'll be all the harder when you've got to face it."

"I don't mind that. A little more freedom, just a little; and then I'll tell her to come to me."

He smoked in silence.

"Surely," I said, "this little more freedom that I ask is a small thing compared with the sacrifice I have promised to make?"

"You won't let her know it's a sacrifice?"

"Of course not. She shall think that I love her as I used to."

"Yes, you ought to do that," he said softly. "Poor devil," he added.

"Am I too selfish?" I asked.

He got up to go. "No," he said. "To my mind, you're entitled to a breathing space before you give up all that you love best. But there's a risk."

"Of what?"

"Of her finding out by some other means than your-self, and before your letter comes, that the letter should have been written earlier. Do you sign all your stuff with your own name?"

"Yes."

"Well, then, she's bound to see how you're getting on. She'll see your name in the magazines, in newspa-pers, and in books. She'll know you don't write for nothing, and she'll make calculations."

I was staggered.

"You mean——?" I said.

"Why, it will occur to her before long that your state-ment of your income doesn't square with the rest of the evidence; and she'll wonder why you pose as a pauper when you're really raking in the money with both hands. She'll think it over, and then she'll see it all."

"I see," I said, dully. "Well, you've taken my last holi-day from me. I'll write to her tonight, telling her the truth."

"I shouldn't, necessarily. Wait a week or two. You may quite possibly hit on some way out of the dif-ficulty. I'm bound to say, though, I can't see one myself at the moment."

"Nor can I," I said.

Chapter 10

TOM BLAKE AGAIN

(James Orlebar Cloyster's narrative continued)

Hatton's Club boys took kindly to my course of instruction. For a couple of months, indeed, it
seemed that another golden age of the noble art was
approaching, and that the rejuvenation of boxing
would occur, beginning at Carnation Hall, Lambeth.

Then the thing collapsed like a punctured tyre.

At first, of course, they fought a little shy. But when
I had them up in line, and had shown them what a
large proportion of an eight-ounce glove is padding,
they grew more at ease. To be asked suddenly to fight
three rounds with one of your friends before an audience, also of your friends, is embarrassing. One feels
hot and uncomfortable. Hatton's boys jibbed ner-
vously. As a preliminary measure, therefore, I drilled
them in a class at foot-work and the left lead. They
found the exercise exhilarating. If this was the idea,
they seemed to say, let the thing go on. Then I showed
them how to be highly scientific with a punch ball. Finally, I sparred lightly with them myself.

In the rough they were impossible boxers. After
their initial distrust had evaporated under my gentle
handling of them, they forgot all I had taught them

about position and guards. They bored in, heads down and arms going like semicircular pistons. Once or twice I had to stop them. They were easily steadied. They hastened to adopt a certain snakiness of attack instead of the frontal method which had left them so exposed. They began to cultivate a kind of negative style. They were tremendously impressed by the superiority of science over strength.

I am not sure that I did not harp rather too much on the scientific note. Perhaps if I had referred to it less, the ultimate disaster would not have been quite so appalling. On the other hand, I had not the slightest suspicion that they would so exaggerate my meaning when I was remarking on the worth of science, how it "tells," and how it causes the meagre stripling to play fast and loose with huge, brawny ruffians—no cowards, mark you—and hairy as to their chests.

But the weeds at Hatton's Club were fascinated by my homilies on science. The simplicity of the thing appealed to them irresistibly. They caught at the expression, "Science," and regarded it as the "Hey Presto!" of a friendly conjurer who could so arrange matters for them that powerful opponents would fall flat, involuntarily, at the sight of their technically correct attitude.

I did not like to destroy their illusions. Had I said to them, "Look here, science is no practical use to you unless you've got low-bridged, snub noses, protruding temples, nostrils like the tubes of a vacuum-cleaner, stomach muscles like motor-car wheels, hands like legs of mutton, and biceps like transatlantic cables"—had I said that, they would have voted boxing a fraud, and gone away to quarrel over a game of backgammon, which was precisely what I wished to avoid.

So I let them go on with their tapping and feinting and side-slipping.

To make it worse they overheard Sidney Price trying

to pay me a compliment. Price was the insurance clerk who had attached himself to Hatton and had proved himself to be of real service in many ways. He was an honest man, but he could not box. He came down to the hall one night after I had given four or five lessons, to watch the boys spar. Of course, to the uninitiated eye it did seem as though they were neat in their work. The sight was very different from the absurd exhibition which Price had seen on the night I started with them. He might easily have said, if he was determined to compliment me, that they had "improved," "progressed," or something equally adequate and innocuous. But no. The man must needs be effusive, positively gushing. He came to me in transports. "Wonderful!" he said. "Wonderful!"

"What's wonderful?" I said, a shade irritably.

"Their style," he said loudly, so that they could all hear, "their style. It's their style that astonishes me."

I hustled him away as soon as I could, but the mischief was done.

Style ran through Hatton's Club boys like an epidemic. Carnation Hall fairly buzzed with style. An apology for a blow which landed on your chest with the delicacy of an Agag among butterflies was extolled to the skies because it was a stylish blow. When Alf Joblin, a recruit, sent Walter Greenway sprawling with a random swing on the mark, there was a pained shudder. Not only Walter Greenway, but the whole club explained to Alf that the swing was a bad swing, an awful violation of style, practically a crime. By the time they had finished explaining, Alf was dazed; and when invited by Walter to repeat the hit with a view to his being further impressed with its want of style, did so in such half-hearted fashion that Walter had time to step stylishly aside and show Alf how futile it is to be unscientific.

To the club this episode was decently buried in an unremembered past. To me, however, it was significant, though I did not imagine it would ever have the tremendous sequel which was brought about by the coming of Thomas Blake.

Fate never planned a coup so successfully. The psychology of Blake's arrival was perfect. The boxers of Carnation Hall had worked themselves into a mental condition which I knew was as ridiculous as it was dangerous. Their conceit and their imagination transformed the hall into a kind of improved National Sporting Club. They went about with an air of subdued but tremendous athleticism. They affected a sort of self-conscious nonchalance. They adopted an odiously patronising attitude towards the once popular game of backgammon. I daresay that picture is not yet forgotten where a British general, a man of blood and iron, is portrayed as playing with a baby, to the utter neglect of a table full of important military dispatches. Well, the club boys, to a boy, posed as generals of blood and iron when they condescended to play backgammon. They did it, but they let you see that they did not regard it as one of the serious things of life.

Also, knowing that each other's hitting was so scientific as to be harmless, they would sometimes deliberately put their eye in front of their opponent's stylish left, in the hope that the blow would raise a bruise. It hardly ever did. But occasionally——! Oh, then you should have seen the hero-with-the-quiet-smile look on their faces as they lounged ostentatiously about the place. In a word, they were above themselves. They sighed for fresh worlds to conquer. And Thomas Blake supplied the long-felt want.

Personally, I did not see his actual arrival. I only saw his handiwork after he had been a visitor awhile within the hall. But, to avoid unnecessary verbiage and to avail myself of the privilege of an author, I will set down, from the evidence of witnesses, the main points of the episode as though I myself had been present at his entrance.

He did not strike them, I am informed, as a particularly big man. He was a shade under average height. His shoulders seemed to them not so much broad as "humpy." He rolled straight in from the street on a wet Saturday night at ten minutes to nine, asking for "free tea."

I should mention that on certain Fridays Hatton gave a free meal to his parishioners on the understanding that it was rigidly connected with a Short Address. The preceding Friday had been such an occasion. The placards announcing the tea were still clinging to the outer railings of the hall.

When I said that Blake asked for free tea, I should have said, shouted for free tea. He cast one decisive glance at Hatton's placards, and rolled up. He shot into the gate, up the steps, down the passage, and through the door leading into the big corrugated-iron hall which I used for my lessons. And all the time he kept shouting for free tea.

In the hall the members of my class were collected. Some were changing their clothes; others, already changed, were tapping the punch-ball. They knew that I always came punctually at nine o'clock, and they liked to be ready for me. Amongst those present was Sidney Price.

Thomas Blake brought up short, hiccuping, in the midst of them. "Gimme that free tea!" he said.

Sidney Price, whose moral fortitude has never been impeached, was the first to handle the situation.

"My good man," he said, "I am sorry to say you have made a mistake."

"A mistake!" said Thomas, quickly taking him up. "A mistake! Oh! What oh! My errer?"

"Quite so," said Price, diplomatically; "an error."

Thomas Blake sat down on the floor, fumbled for a short pipe, and said, "Seems ter me I'm sick of errers. Sick of 'em! Made a bloomer this mornin'—this way." Here he took into his confidence the group which had gathered uncertainly round him. "My wife's brother, 'im wot's a postman, owes me arf a bloomin' thick 'un. 'E's a hard-working bloke, and ter save 'im trouble I came down 'ere from Brentford, where my boat lies, to catch 'im on 'is rounds. Lot of catchin' 'e wanted, too—I *don't* think. Tracked 'im by the knocks at last. And then, wot d'yer think 'e said? Didn't know nothing about no ruddy 'arf thick 'un, and would I kindly cease to impede a public servant in the discharge of 'is dooty. Otherwise—the perlice. That, mind you, was my own brother-in-law. Oh, he's a nice man, I *don't* think!"

Thomas Blake nodded his head as one who, though pained by the hollowness of life, is resigned to it, and proceeded to doze.

The crowd gazed at him and murmured.

Sidney Price, however, stepped forward with authority.

"You'd better be going," he said; and he gently jogged the recumbent boatman's elbow.

"Leave me be! I want my tea," was the muttered and lyrical reply.

"Hook it!" said Price.

"Without my tea?" asked Blake, opening his eyes wide.

"It was yesterday," explained Price, brusquely. "There isn't any free tea tonight."

The effect was magical. A very sinister expression came over the face of the prostrate one, and he slowly clambered to his feet.

"Ho!" he said, disengaging himself from his coat. "Ho. There ain't no free tea ternight, ain't there? Bills stuck on them railings in errer, I suppose. Another bloomin' errer. Seems to me I'm sick of errers. Wot I says is, 'Come on, all of yer.' I'm Tom Blake, I am. You can arst them down at Brentford. Kind old Tom Blake, wot wouldn't hurt a fly; and I says, 'Come on, all of yer,' and I'll knock yer insides through yer backbones."

Sidney Price spoke again. His words were honeyed, but ineffectual.

"I'm honest old Tom, I am," boomed Thomas Blake, "and I'm ready for the lot of yer: you and yer free tea and yer errers."

At this point Alf Joblin detached himself from the hovering crowd and said to Price: "He must be cowed. I'll knock sense into the drunken brute."

"Well," said Price, "he's got to go; but you won't hurt him, Alf, will you?"

"No," said Alf, "I won't hurt him. I'll just make him look a fool. This is where science comes in."

"I'm honest old Tom," droned the boatman.

"If you *will* have it," said Alf, with fine aposiopesis.

He squared up to him.

Now Alf Joblin, like the other pugilists of my class, habitually refrained from delivering any sort of attack until he was well assured that he had seen an orthodox opening. A large part of every round between Hatton's boys was devoted to stealthy circular movements, signifying nothing. But Thomas Blake had not had the advantage of scientific tuition. He came banging in with a sweeping right. Alf stopped him with his left. Again Blake swung his right, and again he took Alf's stopping blow without a blink. Then he went straight in, right and left in quick succession. The force of the right was broken by Alf's guard, but the left got home on the mark; and Alf Joblin's wind left him suddenly. He sat down on the floor.

To say that this tragedy in less than five seconds produced dismay among the onlookers would be incorrect. They were not dismayed. They were amused. They thought that Alf had laid himself open to chaff. Whether he had slipped or lost his head they did not know. But as for thinking that Alf with all his scientific knowledge was not more than a match for this ignorant, intoxicated boatman, such a reflection never entered their heads. What is more, each separate member of the audience was convinced that he individually was the proper person to illustrate the efficacy of style versus untutored savagery.

As soon, therefore, as Alf Joblin went writhing to the floor, and Thomas Blake's voice was raised afresh in a universal challenge, Walter Greenway stepped briskly forward.

And as soon as Walter's guard had been smashed down by a most unconventional attack, and Walter himself had been knocked senseless by a swing on the side of the jaw, Bill Shale leaped gaily forth to take his place.

And so it happened that, when I entered the building at nine, it was as though a devastating tornado had swept down every club boy, sparing only Sidney Price, who was preparing miserably to meet his fate.

To me, standing in the doorway, the situation was plain at the first glance. Only by a big effort could I prevent myself laughing outright. It was impossible to check a grin. Thomas Blake saw me.

"Hullo!" I said; "what's all this?"

He stared at me.

" 'Ullo!" he said, "another of 'em, is it? I'm honest old Tom Blake, *I* am, and wot I say is——"

"Why honest, Mr. Blake?" I interrupted.

"Call me a liar, then!" said he. "Go on. You do it. Call it me, then, and let's see."

He began to shuffle towards me.

"Who pinched his father's trousers, and popped them?" I inquired genially.

He stopped and blinked.

"Eh?" he said weakly.

"And who," I continued, "when sent with twopence to buy postage-stamps, squandered it on beer?"

His jaw dropped, as it had dropped in Covent Garden. It must be very unpleasant to have one's past continually rising up to confront one.

"Look 'ere!" he said, a conciliatory note in his voice, "you and me's pals, mister, ain't we? Say we're pals. Of course we are. You and me don't want no fuss. Of course we don't. Then look here: this is 'ow it is. You come along with me and 'ave a drop."

It did not seem likely that my class would require any instruction in boxing that evening in addition to that which Mr. Blake had given them, so I went with him.

Over the moisture, as he facetiously described it, he grew friendliness itself. He did not ask after Kit, but gave his opinion of her gratuitously. According to him, she was unkind to her relations. "Crool 'arsh," he said. A girl, in fact, who made no allowances for a man, and was over-prone to Sauce and the Nasty Snack.

We parted the best of friends.

"Any time you're on the Cut," he said, gripping my hand with painful fervour, "you look out for Tom Blake, mister. Tom Blake of the *Ashlade* and *Lechton*. No ceremony. Jest drop in on me and the missis. Goo' night."

At the moment of writing Tom Blake is rapidly acquiring an assured position in the heart of the British poetry-loving public. This incident in his career should interest his numerous admirers. The world knows little of its greatest men.

Chapter 11

JULIAN'S IDEA

(James Orlebar Cloyster's narrative continued)

I had been relating, on the morning after the Blake affair, the stirring episode of the previous night to Julian. He agreed with me that it was curious that our potato-thrower of Covent Garden market should have crossed my path again. But I noticed that, though he listened intently enough, he lay flat on his back in his hammock, not looking at me, but blinking at the ceiling; and when I had finished he turned his face towards the wall—which was unusual, since I generally lunched on his breakfast, as I was doing then, to the accompaniment of quite a flow of languid abuse.

I was in particularly high spirits that morning, for I fancied that I had found a way out of my difficulty about Margaret. That subject being uppermost in my mind, I guessed at once what Julian's trouble was.

"I think you'd like to know, Julian," I said, "whether I'd written to Guernsey."

"Well?"

"It's all right," I said.

"You've told her to come?"

"No; but I'm able to take my respite without wounding her. That's as good as writing, isn't it? We agreed on that."

"Yes; that was the idea. If you could find a way of keeping her from knowing how well you were getting on with your writing, you were to take it. What's your idea?"

"I've hit on a very simple way out of the difficulty," I said. "It came to me only this morning. All I need do is to sign my stuff with a pseudonym."

"You only thought of that this morning?"

"Yes. Why?"

"My dear chap, I thought of it as soon as you told me of the fix you were in."

"You might have suggested it."

Julian slid to the floor, drained the almost empty teapot, rescued the last kidney, and began his breakfast.

"I would have suggested it," he said, "if the idea had been worth anything."

"What! What's wrong with it?"

"My dear man, it's too risky. It's not as though you kept to one form of literary work. You're so confoundedly versatile. Let's suppose you did sign your work with a *nom de plume.*"

"Say, George Chandos."

"All right. George Chandos. Well, how long would it be, do you think, before paragraphs appeared, announcing to the public, not only of England but of the Channel Islands, that George Chandos was really Jimmy Cloyster?"

"What rot!" I said. "Why the deuce should they want to write paragraphs about me? I'm not a celebrity. You're talking through your hat, Julian."

Julian lit his pipe.

"Not at all," he said. "Count the number of people who must necessarily be in the secret from the beginning. There are your publishers, Prodder and Way. Then there are the editors of the magazine which publishes your Society dialogue bilge, and of all the news-papers, other than the *Orb,* in which your serious verse appears. My dear Jimmy, the news that you and George Chandos were the same man would go up and down Fleet Street and into the Barrel like wildfire. And after that the paragraphs."

I saw the truth of his reasoning before he had finished speaking. Once more my spirits fell to the point where they had been before I hit upon what I thought was such a bright scheme.

Julian's pipe had gone out while he was talking. He lit it again, and spoke through the smoke:

"The weak point of your idea, of course, is that you and George Chandos are a single individual."

"But why should the editors know that? Why shouldn't I simply send in my stuff, typed, by post, and never appear myself at all?"

"My dear Jimmy, you know as well as I do that that wouldn't work. It would do all right for a bit. Then one morning: 'Dear Mr. Chandos,—I should be glad if you could make it convenient to call here some time between Tuesday and Thursday.—Yours faithfully, Editor of Something-or-other.' Sooner or later a man who writes at all regularly for the papers is bound to meet the editors of them. A successful author can't conduct all his business through the post. Of course, if you chucked London and went to live in the country——"

"I couldn't," I said. "I simply couldn't do it. London's got into my bones."

"It does," said Julian.

"I like the country, but I couldn't live there. Besides, I don't believe I could write there—not for long. All my ideas would go."

Julian nodded.

"Just so," he said. "Then exit George Chandos."

"My scheme is worthless, you think, then?"

"As you state it, yes."

"You mean——?" I prompted quickly, clutching at something in his tone which seemed to suggest that he did not consider the matter entirely hopeless.

"I mean this. The weak spot in your idea, as I told you, is that you and George Chandos have the same body. Now, if you could manage to provide George with separate flesh and blood of his own, there's no reason——"

"By Jove! you've hit it. Go on."

"Listen. Here is my rough draft of what I think might be a sound, working system. How many divisions does your work fall into, not counting the *Orb?*"

I reflected.

"Well, of course, I do a certain amount of odd work, but lately I've rather narrowed it down, and concentrated my output. It seemed to me a better plan than sowing stuff indiscriminately through all the papers in London."

"Well, how many stunts have you got? There's your serious verse—one. And your Society stuff—two. Any more?"

"Novels and short stories."

"Class them together—three. Any more?

"No; that's all."

"Very well, then. What you must do is to look about you, and pick carefully three men on whom you can rely. Divide your signed stuff between these three men. They will receive your copy, sign it with their own names, and see that it gets to wherever you want to send it. As far as the editorial world is concerned, and as far as the public is concerned, they will become actually the authors of the manuscripts which you have prepared for them to sign. They will forward you the cheques when they arrive, and keep accounts to which you will have access. I suppose you will have to pay them a commission on a scale to be fixed by mutual arrangement. As regards your unsigned work, there is nothing to prevent your doing that yourself—'On Your Way,' I mean, whenever there's any holiday work going: general articles, and light verse. I say, though, half a moment."

"Why, what?"

"I've thought of a difficulty. The editors who have been taking your stuff hitherto may have a respect for the name of James Orlebar Cloyster which they may not extend to the name of John Smith or George Chandos, or whoever it is. I mean, it's quite likely the withdrawal of the name will lead to the rejection of the manuscript."

"Oh no; that's all right," I said. "It's the stuff they want, not the name. I don't say that names don't matter. They do. But only if they're big names. Kipling might get a story rejected if he sent it in under a false name, which they'd have taken otherwise just because he was Kipling. What they want from me is the goods. I can shove any label on them I like. The editor will read my ghosts' stuff, see it's what he wants, and put it in. He may say, 'It's rather like Cloyster's style,' but he'll certainly add, 'Anyhow, it's what I want.' You can scratch that difficulty, Julian. Any more?"

"I think not. Of course, there's the objection that you'll lose any celebrity you might have got. No one'll say, 'Oh, Mr. Cloyster, I enjoyed your last book so much!' "

"And no one'll say, 'Oh, do you *write*, Mr. Cloyster? How interesting! What have you written? You must send me a copy.' "

"That's true. In any case, it's celebrity against the respite, obscurity against Miss Goodwin. While the system is in operation you will be free but inglorious. You choose freedom? All right, then. Pass the matches."

Chapter 12

THE FIRST GHOST

(James Orlebar Cloyster's narrative continued)

Such was the suggestion Julian made; and I praised its ingenuity, little thinking how bitterly I should come to curse it in the future.

I was immediately all anxiety to set the scheme working.

"Will you be one of my three middlemen, Julian?" I asked.

He shook his head.

"Thanks!" he said; "it's very good of you, but I daren't encroach further on my hours of leisure. Skeffington's Sloe Gin has already become an incubus."

I could not move him from this decision.

It is not everybody who, in a moment of emergency, can put his hand on three men of his acquaintance capable of carrying through a more or less delicate business for him. Certainly I found a difficulty in making my selection. I ran over the list of my friends in my mind. Then I was compelled to take pencil and paper, and settle down seriously to what I now saw would be a task of some difficulty. After half an hour I read through my list, and could not help smiling. I had indeed a mixed lot of acquaintances. First came Julian and

Malim, the two pillars of my world. I scratched them out. Julian had been asked and had refused; and, as for Malim, I shrank from exposing my absurd compositions to his critical eye. A man who could deal so trenchantly over a pipe and a whisky-and-soda with Established Reputations would hardly take kindly to seeing my work in print under his name. I wished it had been possible to secure him, but I did not disguise it from myself that it was not.

The rest of the list was made up of members of the Barrel Club (impossible because of their inherent tendency to break out into personal paragraphs); writers like Fermin and Gresham, above me on the literary ladder, and consequently unapproachable in a matter of this kind; certain college friends, who had vanished into space, as men do on coming down from the 'Varsity, leaving no address; John Hatton, Sidney Price, and Tom Blake.

There were only three men in that list to whom I felt I could take my suggestion. Hatton was one, Price was another, and Blake was the third. Hatton should have my fiction, Price my Society stuff, Blake my serious verse.

That evening I went off to the Temple to sound Hatton on the subject of signing my third book. The wretched sale of my first two had acted as something of a check to my enthusiasm for novel-writing. I had paused to take stock of my position. My first two novels had, I found on re-reading them, too much of the 'Varsity tone in them to be popular. That is the mistake a man falls into through being at Cambridge or Oxford. He fancies unconsciously that the world is peopled with undergraduates. He forgets that what appeals to an undergraduate public may be Greek to the outside reader—and, unfortunately, not compulsory Greek. The reviewers had dealt kindly with my two

books ("this pleasant little squib," "full of quiet humour," "should amuse all who remember their undergraduate days"); but the great heart of the public had
remained untouched, as had the great purse of the
public. I had determined to adopt a different style.
And now my third book was ready. It was called, *When
It Was Lurid,* with the sub-title, *A Tale of God and Allah.*
There was a piquant admixture of love, religion, and
Eastern scenery which seemed to point to a record
number of editions.

I took the type-script of this book with me to the
Temple.

Hatton was in. I flung *When It Was Lurid* on the
table, and sat down.

"What's this?" inquired Hatton, fingering the brown-
paper parcel. "If it's the corpse of a murdered editor, I
think it's only fair to let you know that I have a preju-
dice against having my rooms used as a cemetery. Go
and throw him into the river."

"It's anything but a corpse. It's the most lively bit of
writing ever done. There's enough fire in that book to
singe your tablecloth."

"You aren't going to read it to me out loud?" he said
anxiously.

"No."

"Have I got to read it when you're gone?"

"Not unless you wish to."

"Then why, if I may ask, do you carry about a parcel
which, I should say, weighs anything between one and
two tons, simply to use it as a temporary table ornament? Is it the Sandow System?"

"No," I said; "it's like this."

And suddenly it dawned on me that it was not going
to be particularly easy to explain to Hatton just what it
was that I wanted him to do.

I made the thing clear at last, suppressing, of course,

my reasons for the move. When he had grasped my meaning, he looked at me rather curiously.

"Doesn't it strike you," he said, "that what you propose is slightly dishonourable?"

"You mean that I have come deliberately to insult you, Hatton?"

"Our conversation seems to be getting difficult, unless you grant that honour is not one immovable, intangible landmark, fixed for humanity, but that it is a commodity we all carry with us in varying forms."

"Personally, I believe that, as a help to identification, honour-impressions would be as useful as fingerprints."

"Good! You agree with me. Now, you may have a different view; but, in my opinion, if I were to pose as the writer of your books, and gained credit for a literary skill——"

I laughed.

"You won't get credit for literary skill out of the sort of books I want you to put your name to. They're potboilers. You needn't worry about Fame. You'll be a martyr, not a hero."

"You may be right. You wrote the book. But, in any case, I should be more of a charlatan than I care about."

"You won't do it?" I said. "I'm sorry. It would have been a great convenience to me."

"On the other hand," continued Hatton, ignoring my remark, "there are arguments in favour of such a scheme as you suggest."

"Stout fellow!" I said encouragingly.

"To examine the matter in its—er—financial—to suppose for a moment—briefly, what do I get out of it?"

"Ten per cent."

He looked thoughtful.

"The end shall justify the means," he said. "The money you pay me can do something to help the awful, the continual poverty of Lambeth. Yes, James Cloyster, I will sign whatever you send me."

"Good for you," I said.

"And I shall come better out of the transaction than you."

No one would credit the way that man—a clergyman, too—haggled over terms. He ended by squeezing fifteen per cent out of me.

Chapter 13

THE SECOND GHOST

(*James Orlebar Cloyster's narrative continued*)

The reasons which had led me to select Sidney Price as the sponsor of my Society dialogues will be immediately apparent to those who have read them. They were just the sort of things you would expect an insurance clerk to write. The humour was thin, the satire as cheap as the papers in which they appeared, and the vulgarity in exactly the right quantity for a public that ate it by the pound and asked for more. Everything pointed to Sidney Price as the man.

It was my intention to allow each of my three ghosts to imagine that he was alone in the business; so I did not get Price's address from Hatton, who might have wondered why I wanted it, and had suspicions. I applied to the doorkeeper at Carnation Hall; and on the following evening I rang the front-door bell of The Hollyhocks, Belmont Park Road, Brixton.

Whilst I was waiting on the step, I was able to get a view through the slats of the Venetian blind of the front ground-floor sitting-room. I could scarcely restrain a cry of pure æsthetic delight at what I saw within. Price was sitting on a horse-hair sofa with an arm round the waist of a rather good-looking girl. Her eyes were fixed on his. It was Edwin and Angelina in real life.

Up till then I had suffered much discomfort from the illustrated record of their adventures in the comic papers. "Is there really," I had often asked myself, "a body of men so gifted that they can construct the impossible details of the lives of nonexistent types purely from imagination? If such creative genius as theirs is unrecognized and ignored, what hope of recognition is there for one's own work?" The thought had frequently saddened me; but here at last they were— Edwin and Angelina in the flesh!

I took the gallant Sidney for a fifteen-minute stroll up and down the length of the Belmont Park Road. Poor Angelina! He came, as he expressed it, "like a bird." Give him a sec. to slip on a pair of boots, he said, and he would be with me in two ticks.

He was so busy getting his hat and stick from the stand in the passage that he quite forgot to tell the lady that he was going out, and, as we left, I saw her with the tail of my eye sitting stolidly on the sofa, still wearing patiently the expression of her comic-paper portraits.

The task of explaining was easier than it had been with Hatton.

"Sorry to drag you out, Price," I said, as we went down the steps.

"Don't mention it, Mr. Cloyster," he said. "Norah won't mind a bit of a sit by herself. Looked in to have a chat, or is there anything I can do?"

"It's like this," I said. "You know I write a good deal?"

"Yes."

"Well, it has occurred to me that, if I go on turning out quantities of stuff under my own name, there's a danger of the public getting tired of me."

He nodded.

"Now, I'm with you there, mind you," he said. " 'Can't have too much of a good thing,' some chaps say. I say, 'Yes, you can.' Stands to reason a chap can't go on writing and writing without making a bloomer every now and then. What he wants is to take his time over it. Look at all the real swells—'Erbert Spencer, Marie Corelli, and what not—you don't find them pushing it out every day of the year. They wait a bit and have a look round, and then they start again when they're ready. Stands to reason that's the only way."

"Quite right," I said; "but the difficulty, if you live by writing, is that you must turn out a good deal, or you don't make enough to live on. I've got to go on getting stuff published, but I don't want people to be always seeing my name about."

"You mean, adopt a *nom de ploom?*"

"That's the sort of idea; but I'm going to vary it a little."

And I explained my plan.

"But why me?" he asked, when he had understood the scheme. "What made you think of me?"

"The fact is, my dear fellow," I said, "this writing is a game where personality counts to an enormous extent. The man who signs my Society dialogues will probably come into personal contact with the editors of the papers in which they appear. He will be asked to call at their offices. So you see I must have a man who looks as if he had written the stuff."

"I see," he said complacently. "Dressy sort of chap. Chap who looks as if he knew a thing or two."

"Yes. I couldn't get Alf Joblin, for instance."

We laughed together at the notion.

"Poor old Alf!" said Sidney Price.

"Now you probably know a good deal about Society?"

"Rath*er!*" said Sidney. "They're a hot lot. My *word!* Saw *The Walls of Jericho* three times. Gives it 'em pretty straight, that does. *Visits of Elizabeth,* too. Chase me! Used to think some of us chaps in the 'Moon' were a bit O.T., but we aren't in it—not in the same street. Chaps, I mean, who'd call a girl behind the bar by her Christian name as soon as look at you. One chap I knew used to give the girl at the cash-desk of the 'Mecca' he went to bottles of scent. Bottles of it—regular! 'Here you are, Tottie,' he used to say, 'here's another little donation from yours truly.' Kissed her once. Slap in front of everybody. Saw him do it. But, bless you, they'd think nothing of that in the Smart Set. Ever read 'God's Good Man'? There's a book! My stars! Lets you see what goes on. Scorchers they are."

"That's just what my dialogues point out. I can count on you, then?"

He said I could. He was an intelligent young man, and he gave me to understand that all would be well. He would carry the job through on the strict Q.T. He closely willingly with my offer of ten per cent, thus affording a striking contrast to the grasping Hatton. He assured me he had found literary chaps not half bad. Had occasionally had an idea of writing a bit himself.

We parted on good terms, and I was pleased to think that I was placing my "Dialogues of Mayfair" and my "London and Country House Tales" in really competent and appreciative hands.

Chapter 14

THE THIRD GHOST

(James Orlebar Cloyster's narrative continued)

There only remained now my serious verse, of which I turned out an enormous quantity. It won a ready acceptance in many quarters, notably the *St. Stephen's Gazette*. Already I was beginning to oust from their positions on that excellent journal the old crusted poetesses who had supplied it from its foundation with verse. The prices they paid on the *St. Stephen's* were in excellent taste. In the musical world, too, I was making way rapidly. Lyrics of the tea-and-muffin type streamed from my pen. "Sleep whilst I Sing, Love," had brought me in an astonishing amount of money, in spite of the music-pirates. It was on the barrel-organs. Adults hummed it. Infants crooned it in their cots. Comic men at music-halls opened their turns by remarking soothingly to the conductor of the orchestra, "I'm going to sing now, so you go to sleep, love." In a word, while the boom lasted, it was a little gold-mine to me.

Thomas Blake was as obviously the man for me here as Sidney Price had been in the case of my Society dialogues. The public would find something infinitely piquant in the thought that its most sentimental ditties were given to it by the horny-handed steerer of a canal barge. He would be greeted as the modern Burns. People would ask him how he thought of his poems, and he would say, "Oo-er!" and they would hail him as delightfully original. In the case of Thomas Blake I saw my earnings going up with a bound. His personality would be a noble advertisement.

He was aboard the *Ashlade* or *Lechton* on the Cut, so I was informed by Kit. Which information was not luminous to me. Further inquiries, however, led me to the bridge at Brentford, whence starts that almost unknown system of inland navigation which extends to Manchester and Birmingham.

Here I accosted at a venture a ruminative bargee. "Tom Blake?" he repeated, reflectively. "Oh! 'e's been off this three hours on a trip to Braunston. He'll tie up tonight at the Shovel."

"Where's the Shovel?"

"Past Cowley, the Shovel is." This was spoken in a tired drawl which was evidently meant to preclude further chit-chat. To clinch things, he slouched away, waving me in an abstracted manner to the towpath.

I took the hint. It was now three o'clock in the afternoon. Judging by the pace of the barges I had seen, I should catch Blake easily before nightfall. I set out briskly. An hour's walking brought me to Hanwell, and I was glad to see a regular chain of locks which must have considerably delayed the *Ashlade* and *Lechton*.

The afternoon wore on. I went steadily forward, making inquiries as to Thomas's whereabouts from the boats which met me, and always hearing that he was still ahead.

Footsore and hungry, I overtook him at Cowley. The two boats were in the lock. Thomas and a lady, presumably his wife, were ashore. On the *Ashlade*'s raised cabin cover was a baby. Two patriarchal-looking boys were respectively at the *Ashlade*'s and *Lechton*'s tillers. The lady was attending to the horse.

The water in the lock rose gradually to a higher level.

"Hold them tillers straight!" yelled Thomas. At which point I saluted him. He was a little blank at first, but when I reminded him of our last meeting his face lit up at once. "Why, you're the mister wot——"

"Nuppie!" came in a shrill scream from the lady with the horse. "Nuppie!"

"Yes, Ada!" answered the boy on the *Ashlade*.

"Liz ain't tied to the can. D'you want 'er to be drownded? Didn't I tell you to be sure and tie her up tight?"

"So I did, Ada. She's untied herself again. Yes, she 'as. 'Asn't she, Albert?"

This appeal for corroboration was directed to the other small boy on the *Lechton*. It failed signally.

"No, you did not tie Liz to the chimney. You know you never, Nuppie."

"Wait till we get out of this lock!" said Nuppie, earnestly.

The water pouring in from the northern sluice was forcing the tillers violently against the southern sluice gates.

"If them boys," said Tom Blake in an overwrought voice, "lets them tillers go round, it's all up with my pair o' boats. Lemme do it, you——" The rest of the sentence was mercifully lost in the thump with which Thomas's feet bounded on the *Ashlade*'s cabin-top. He made Liz fast to the circular foot of iron chimney projecting from the boards; then, jumping back to the land, he said, more in sorrow than in anger: "Lazy little brats! an' they've 'ad their tea, too."

Clear of the locks, I walked with Thomas and his ancient horse, trying to explain what I wanted done. But it was not until we had tied up for the night, had had beer at the Shovel, and (Nuppie and Albert being safely asleep in the second cabin) had met at supper that my instructions had been fully grasped. Thomas himself was inclined to be diffident, and had it not been for Ada would, I think, have let my offer slide. She was enthusiastic. It was she who told me of the cottage they had at Fenny Stratford, which they used as headquarters whilst waiting for a cargo.

"That can be used as a permanent address," I said. "All you have to do is to write your name at the end of each typewritten sheet, enclose it in the stamped envelope which I will send you, and send it by post. When the cheques come, sign them on the back and forward them to me. For every ten pounds you forward me, I'll give you one for yourself. In any difficulty, simply write to me—here's my own address—and I'll see you through it."

"We can't go to prison for it, can we, mister?" asked Ada suddenly, after a pause.

"No," I said; "there's nothing dishonest in what I propose."

"Oh, she didn't so much mean that," said Thomas, thoughtfully.

They gave me a shakedown for the night in the cargo.

Just before turning in, I said casually, "If anyone except me cashed the cheques by mistake, he'd go to prison quick."

"Yes, mister," came back Thomas's voice, again a shade thoughtfully modulated.

Chapter 15

EVA EVERSLEIGH

(James Orlebar Cloyster's narrative continued)

With my system thus in full swing I experienced the intoxication of assured freedom. To say I was elated does not describe it. I walked on air. This was my state of mind when I determined to pay a visit to the Gunton-Cresswells. I had known them in my college days, but since I had been engaged in literature I had sedulously avoided them because I remembered that Margaret had once told me they were her friends.

But now there was no need for me to fear them on that account, and thinking that the solid comfort of their house in Kensington would be far from disagreeable, thither, one afternoon in spring, I made my way. It is wonderful how friendly Convention is to Art when Art does not appear to want to borrow money.

No. 5, Kensington Lane, W., is the stronghold of British respectability. It is more respectable than the most respectable suburb. Its attitude to Mayfair is that of a mother to a daughter who has gone on the stage and made a success. Kensington Lane is almost tolerant of Mayfair. But not quite. It admits the success, but shakes its head.

Mrs. Gunton-Cresswell took an early opportunity of

drawing me aside, and began gently to pump me. After I had responded with sufficient docility to her leads, she reiterated her delight at seeing me again. I had concluded my replies with the words, "I am a struggling journalist, Mrs. Cresswell." I accompanied the phrase with a half-smile which she took to mean—as I intended she should—that I was amusing myself by dabbling in literature, backed by a small, but adequate, private income.

"Oh, come, James," she said, smiling approvingly, "you know you will make a quite too dreadfully clever success. How dare you try to deceive me like that? A struggling journalist, indeed."

But I knew she liked that "struggling journalist" immensely. She would couple me and my own epithet together before her friends. She would enjoy unconsciously an imperceptible, but exquisite, sensation of patronage by having me at her house. Even if she discussed me with Margaret I was safe. For Margaret would give an altogether different interpretation of the smile with which I described myself as struggling. My smile would be mentally catalogued by her as "brave"; for it must not be forgotten that as suddenly as my name had achieved a little publicity, just so suddenly had it utterly disappeared.

Towards the end of May, it happened that Julian dropped into my rooms about three o'clock, and found me gazing critically at a top-hat.

"I've seen you," he remarked, "rather often in that get-up lately."

"It *is*, perhaps, losing its first gloss," I answered, inspecting my hat closely. I cared not a bit for Julian's sneers; for the smell of the flesh-pots of Kensington had laid hold of my soul, and I was resolved to make the most of the respite which my system gave me.

"What salon is to have the honour today?" he asked, spreading himself on my sofa.

"I'm going to the Gunton-Cresswells," I replied.

Julian slowly sat up.

"Ah?" he said conversationally.

"I've been asked to meet their niece, a Miss Eversleigh, whom they've invited to stop with them. Funny, by the way, that her name should be the same as yours."

"Not particularly," said Julian shortly; "she's my cousin. My cousin Eva."

This was startling. There was a pause. Presently Julian said, "Do you know, Jimmy, that if I were not the philosopher I am, I'd curse this awful indolence of mine."

I saw it in a flash, and went up to him holding out my hand in sympathy. "Thanks," he said, gripping it; "but don't speak of it. I couldn't endure that, even from you, James. It's too hard for talking. If it was only myself whose life I'd spoilt—if it was only myself——"

He broke off. And then, "Hers too. She's true as steel."

I had heard no more bitter cry than that.

I began to busy myself amongst some manuscripts to give Julian time to compose himself. And so an hour passed. At a quarter past four I got up to go out. Julian lay recumbent. It seemed terrible to leave him brooding alone over his misery.

A closer inspection, however, showed me he was asleep.

Meanwhile, Eva Eversleigh and I became firm friends. Of her person I need simply say that it was the most beautiful that Nature ever created. Pressed as to details, I should add that she was *petite,* dark, had brown hair, very big blue eyes, a *retroussé* nose, and a rather wide mouth.

Julian had said she was "true as steel." Therefore, I felt no diffidence in manœuvring myself into her society on every conceivable occasion. Sometimes she spoke to me of Julian, whom I admitted I knew, and, with feminine courage, she hid her hopeless, all-devouring affection for her cousin under the cloak of ingenuous levity. She laughed nearly every time his name was mentioned.

About this time the Gunton-Cresswells gave a dance.

I looked forward to it with almost painful pleasure. I had not been to a dance since my last May-week at Cambridge. Also No. 5, Kensington Lane had completely usurped the position I had previously assigned to Paradise. To waltz with Julian's cousin—that was the ambition which now dwarfed my former hankering for the fame of authorship or a habitation in Bohemia.

Mrs. Goodwin once said that happiness consists in anticipating an impossible future. Be that as it may, I certainly thought my sensations were pleasant enough when at length my hansom pulled up jerkily beside the red-carpeted steps of No. 5, Kensington Lane. As I paid the fare, I could hear the murmur from within of a waltz tune—and I kept repeating to myself that Eva had promised me the privilege of taking her in to supper, and had given me the last two waltzes and the first two extras.

I went to pay my *devoirs* to my hostess. She was supinely gamesome. "Ah," she said, showing her excellent teeth, "Genius attendant at the revels of Terpsichore."

"Where Beauty, Mrs. Gunton-Cresswell," I responded, cutting it, as though mutton, thick, "teaches e'en the humblest visitor the reigning Muse's art."

"You may have this one, if you like," said Mrs. Gunton-Cresswell simply.

Supper came at last, and, with supper, Eva.

I must now write it down that she was not a type of English beauty. She was not, I mean, queenly, impassive, never-anything-but-her-cool-calm-self. Tonight, for instance, her eyes were as I had never seen them. There danced in them the merriest glitter, which was more than a mere glorification of the ordinary merry glitter—which scores of girls possess at every ball. To begin with, there was a diabolical abandon in Eva's glitter, which raised it instantly above the common herd's. And behind it all was that very misty mist. I don't know whether all men have seen that mist; but I am sure that no man has seen it more than once; and, from what I've seen of the average man, I doubt if most of them have ever seen it at all. Well, there it was for me to see in Eva Eversleigh's eyes that night at supper. It made me think of things unspeakable. I felt a rush of classic æstheticism: Arcadia, Helen of Troy, the happy valleys of the early Greeks. Supper! I believe I gave her oyster *pâtés*. But I was far away. Deep, deep, deep in Eva's eyes I saw a craft sighting, 'neath a cloudless azure sky, the dark blue Symplegades; heard in my ears the jargon, loud and near me, of the sailors; and faintly o'er the distance of the dead-calm sea rose intermittently the sound of brine-foam at the clashing rocks. . . .

As we sat there *tête-à-tête*, she smiled across the table at me with such perfect friendliness, it seemed as though a magic barrier separated our two selves from all the chattering, rustling crowd around us. When she spoke, a little quiver of feeling blended adorably with the low, sweet tones of her voice. We talked, indeed, of trifles, but with just that charming hint of intimacy

which men friends have who may have known one
another from birth, and may know one another for a
lifetime, but never become bores, never change. Only
when it comes between a woman and a man, it is in-
comparably finer. It is the talk, of course, of lovers who
have not realised they are in love.

"The two last waltzes," I murmured, when parting
with her. She nodded. I roamed the Gunton-
Cresswells's rooms awaiting them.

She danced those two last waltzes with strangers.

The thing was utterly beyond me at the time. Looking back, I am still amazed to what lengths deliberate
coquetry can go.

She actually took pains to elude me, and gave those
waltzes to strangers.

From being comfortably rocked in the dark blue
waters of a Grecian sea, I was suddenly transported to
the realities of the ballroom. My theoretical love for
Eva was now a substantial truth. I was in an agony of
desire, in a frenzy of jealousy. I wanted to hurl the two
strangers to opposite corners of the ballroom, but civi-
lisation forbade it.

I was now in an altogether indescribable state of
nerves and suspense. Had she definitely and for some
unfathomable reason decided to cut me? The first
extra drew languorously to a close, couples swept from
the room to the grounds, the gallery or the conservatory. I tried to steady my whirling head with a cigarette
and a whisky-and-soda in the smoking-room.

The orchestra, like a train starting tentatively on a
long run, launched itself mildly into the preliminary
bars of *Tout Passe*. I sought the ballroom blinded by
my feelings. Pulling myself together with an effort, I
saw her standing alone. It struck me for the first time
that she was clothed in cream. Her skin gleamed shin-

ing white. She stood erect, her arms by her sides. Behind her was a huge, black velvet *portière* of many folds, supported by two dull brazen columns.

As I advanced towards her, two or three men bowed and spoke to her. She smiled and dismissed them, and, still smiling pleasantly, her glance traversed the crowd and rested upon me. I was drawing now quite near. Her eyes met mine; nor did she avert them, and stooping a little to address her, I heard her sigh.

"You're tired," I said, forgetting my two last dances, forgetting everything but that I loved her.

"Perhaps I am," she said, taking my arm. We turned in silence to the *portière* and found ourselves in the hall. The doors were opened. Some servants were there. At the bottom of the steps I chanced to see a yellow light.

"Find out if that cab's engaged," I said to a footman.

"The cool air——" I said to Eva.

"The cab is not engaged, sir," said the footman, returning.

"Yes," said Eva, in answer to my glance.

"Drive to the corner of Sloane Street, by way of the Park," I told the driver.

I have said that I had forgotten everything except that I loved her. Could it help remembrance now that we two sped alone through empty streets, her warm, palpitating body touching mine?

Julian, his friendship for me, his love for Eva; Margaret and her love for me; my own honour—these things were blotted from my brain.

"Eva!" I murmured; and I took her hand.

"Eva."

Her wonderful eyes met mine. The mist in them seemed to turn to dew.

"My darling," she whispered, very low. And, the road being deserted, I drew her face to mine and kissed her.

Chapter 16

I TELL JULIAN

(James Orlebar Cloyster's narrative continued)

Is any man really honourable? I wonder. Hundreds, thousands go triumphantly through life with that reputation. But how far is this due to absence of temptation? Life, which is like cricket in so many ways, resembles the game in this also. A batsman makes a century, and, having made it, is bowled by a ball which he is utterly unable to play. What if that ball had come at the beginning of his innings instead of at the end of it? Men go through life without a stain on their honour. I wonder if it simply means that they had the luck not to have the good ball bowled to them early in their innings. To take my own case. I had always considered myself a man of honour. I had a code that was rigid compared with that of a large number of men. In theory I should never have swerved from it. I was fully prepared to carry out my promise and marry Margaret, at the expense of my happiness—until I met Eva. I would have done anything to avoid injuring Julian, my friend, until I met Eva. Eva was my temptation, and I fell. Nothing in the world mattered, so that she was mine. I ought to have had a revulsion of feeling as I walked back to my rooms in Walpole Street.

The dance was over. The music had ceased. The dawn was chill. And at a point midway between Kensington Lane and the Brompton Oratory I had proposed to Eversleigh's cousin, his Eva, "true as steel," and had been accepted.

Yet I had no remorse. I did not even try to justify my behaviour to Julian or to Margaret, or—for she must suffer, too—to Mrs. Gunton-Cresswell, who, I knew well, was socially ambitious for her niece.

To all these things I was indifferent. I repeated softly to myself, "We love each other."

From this state of coma, however, I was aroused by the appearance of my window-blind. I saw, in fact, that my room was illuminated. Remembering that I had been careful to put out my lamp before I left, I feared, as I opened the hall door, a troublesome encounter with a mad housebreaker. Mad, for no room such as mine could attract a burglar who has even the slightest pretensions to sanity.

It was not a burglar. It was Julian Eversleigh, and he was lying asleep on my sofa.

There was nothing peculiar in this. I roused him.

"Julian," I said.

"I'm glad you're back," he said, sitting up; "I've some news for you."

"So have I," said I. For I had resolved to tell him what I had done.

"Hear mine first. It's urgent. Miss Margaret Goodwin has been here."

My heart seemed to leap.

"Today?" I cried.

"Yes. I had called to see you, and was waiting a little while on the chance of your coming in when I happened to look out of the window. A girl was coming down the street, looking at the numbers of the houses. She stopped here. Intuition told me she was Miss

Goodwin. While she was ringing the bell I did all I could to increase the shabby squalor of your room. She was shown in here, and I introduced myself as your friend. We chatted. I drew an agonising picture of your struggle for existence. You were brave, talented, and unsuccessful. Though you went often hungry, you had a plucky smile upon your lips. It was a meritorious bit of work. Miss Goodwin cried a good deal. She is charming. I was so sorry for her that I laid it on all the thicker."

"Where is she now?"

"Nearing Guernsey. She's gone."

"Gone!" I said. "Without seeing me! I don't understand."

"You don't understand how she loves you, James."

"But she's gone. Gone without a word."

"She has gone because she loved you so. She had intended to stay with the Gunton-Cresswells. She knows them, it seems. They didn't know she was coming. She didn't know herself until this morning. She happened to be walking on the quay at St. Peter's Port. The outward-bound boat was on the point of starting for England. A wave of affection swept over Miss Goodwin. She felt she must see you. Scribbling a note, which she despatched to her mother, she went aboard. She came straight here. Then, when I had finished with her, when I had lied consistently about you for an hour, she told me she must return. 'I must not see James,' she said. 'You have torn my heart. I should break down.' And she said, speaking, I think, half to herself, 'Your courage is so noble, so different from mine. And I must not impose a needless strain upon it. You shall not see me weep for you.' And then she went away."

Julian's voice broke. He was genuinely affected by his own recital.

For my part, I saw that I had bludgeon work to do.

It is childish to grumble at the part Fate forces one to play. Sympathetic or otherwise, one can only enact one's *rôle* to the utmost of one's ability. Mine was now essentially unsympathetic, but I was determined that it should be adequately played.

I went to the fireplace and poked the fire into a blaze. Then, throwing my hat on the table and lighting a cigarette, I regarded Julian cynically.

"You're a nice sort of person, aren't you?" I said.

"What do you mean?" asked Julian, startled, as I had meant that he should be, by the question.

I laughed.

"Aren't you just a little transparent, my dear Julian?"

He stared blankly.

I took up a position in front of the fire.

"Disloyalty," I said tolerantly, "where a woman is concerned, is in the eyes of some people almost a negative virtue."

"I don't know what on earth you're talking about."

"Don't you?"

I was sorry for him all the time. In a curiously impersonal way I could realise the depths to which I was sinking in putting this insult upon him. But my better feelings were gagged and bound that night. The one thought uppermost in my mind was that I must tell Julian of Eva, and that by his story of Margaret he had given me an opening for making my confession with the minimum of discomfort to myself.

It was pitiful to see the first shaft of my insinuation slowly sink into him. I could see by the look in his eyes that he had grasped my meaning.

"Jimmy," he gasped, "you can't think—are you joking?"

"I am not surprised at your asking that question," I replied pleasantly. "You know how tolerant I am. But

I'm not joking. Not that I blame you, my dear fellow. Margaret is, or used to be, very good-looking."

"You seem to be in earnest," he said, in a dazed way.

"My dear fellow," I said; "I have a certain amount of intuition. You spend an hour here alone with Margaret. She is young, and very pretty. You are placed immediately on terms of intimacy by the fact that you have, in myself, a subject of mutual interest. That breaks the ice. You are at cross-purposes, but your main sympathies are identical. Also, you have a strong objective sympathy for Margaret. I think we may presuppose that this second sympathy is stronger than the first. It pivots on a woman, not on a man. And on a woman who is present, not on a man who is absent. You see my meaning? At any rate, the solid fact remains that she stayed an hour with you, whom she had met for the first time today, and did not feel equal to meeting me, whom she has loved for two years. If you want me to explain myself further, I have no objection to doing so. I mean that you made love to her."

I watched him narrowly to see how he would take it. The dazed expression deepened on his face.

"You are apparently sane," he said, very wearily. "You seem to be sober."

"I am both," I said.

There was a pause.

"It's no use for me," he began, evidently collecting his thoughts with a strong effort, "to say your charge is preposterous. I don't suppose mere denial would convince you. I can only say, instead, that the charge is too wild to be replied to except in one way, which is this. Employ for a moment your own standard of right and wrong. I know your love story, and you know mine. Miss Eversleigh, my cousin, is to me what Miss Goodwin is to you—true as steel. My loyalty and my friendship for you are the same as your loyalty and your friendship for me."

"Well?"

"Well, if I have spent an hour with Miss Goodwin, you have spent more than an hour with my cousin. What right have you to suspect me more than I have to suspect you? Judge me by your own standard."

"I do," I said, "and I find myself still suspecting you."

He stared.

"I don't understand you."

"Perhaps you will when you have heard the piece of news which I mentioned earlier in our conversation that I had for you."

"Well?"

"I proposed to your cousin at the Gunton-Cresswells's dance tonight, and she accepted me."

The news had a surprising effect on Julian. First he blinked. Then he craned his head forward in the manner of a deaf man listening with difficulty.

Then he left the room without a word.

He had not been gone two minutes when there were three short, sharp taps at my window.

Julian returned? Impossible. Yet who else could have called on me at that hour?

I went to the front door, and opened it.

On the steps stood the Rev. John Hatton. Beside him Sidney Price. And, lurking in the background, Tom Blake of the *Ashlade* and *Lechton*.

(End of James Orlebar Cloyster's narrative.)

Sidney Price's Narrative

Chapter 17

A GHOSTLY GATHERING

Norah Perkins is a peach, and I don't care who knows it; but, all the same, there's no need to tell her every little detail of a man's past life. Not that I've been a Don What's-his-name. Far from it. Costs a bit too much, that game. You simply can't do it on sixty quid a year, paid monthly, and that's all there is about it. Not but what I don't often think of going it a bit when things are slack at the office and my pal in the New Business Department is out for lunch. It's the loneliness makes you think of going a regular plunger. More than once, when Tommy Milner hasn't been there to talk to, I tell you I've half a mind to take out some girl or other to tea at the "Cabin." I have, straight.

Yet somehow when the assist. cash. comes round with the wicker tray on the 1st, and gives you the envelope ("Mr. Price") and you take out the five sovereigns—well, somehow, there's such a lot of other things which you don't want to buy but have just got to. Tommy Milner said the other day, and I quite agree with him, "When I took my clean handkerchief out last fortnight," he said, "I couldn't help totting up what a lot I spend on trifles." That's it. There you've got it in a nutshell. Washing, bootlaces, 'bus-tickets—trifles, in fact: that's where the coin goes. Only the other morning I bust my braces. I was late already, and pinning them together all but lost me the 9:16, only it was a bit behind time. It struck me then as I ran to the station that the average person would never count braces an expense. Trifles—that's what it is.

No; I may have smoked a cig. too much and been so chippy next day that I had to go out and get a cup of tea at the A.B.C.; or I may now and again have gone up West of an evening for a bit of a look round; but beyond that I've never been really what you'd call vicious. Very likely it's been my friendship for Mr. Hatton that's curbed me breaking out as I've sometimes imagined myself doing when I've been alone in the New Business Room. Though I must say, in common honesty to myself, that there's always been the fear of getting the sack from the "Moon." The "Moon" isn't like some other insurance companies I could mention which'll take anyone. Your refs. must be A1, or you don't stand an earthly. Simply not an earthly. Besides, the "Moon" isn't an Insurance Company at all: it's an *As*surance Company. Of course, now I've chucked the "Moon" ("shot the moon," as Tommy Milner, who's the office comic, put it) and taken to Literature I could do pretty well what I liked, if it weren't for Norah.

Which brings me back to what I was saying just now—that I'm not sure whether I shall tell her the Past. I may and I may not. I'll have to think it over. Anyway, I'm going to write it down first and see how it looks. If it's all right it can go into my autobiography. If it isn't, then I shall lie low about it. That's the posish.

It all started from my friendship with Mr. Hatton— the Rev. Mr. Hatton. If it hadn't have been for that man I should still be working out rates of percentage for the "Moon" and listening to Tommy Milner's so-called witticisms. Of course, I've cut him now. A literary man, a man who supplies the *Strawberry Leaf* with two columns of Social Interludes at a salary I'm not going to mention in case Norah gets to hear of it and wants to lash out, a man whose Society novels are competed for by every publisher in London and New York—well, can a man in that position be expected to keep up with an impudent little ledger-lugger like Tommy Milner? It can't be done.

I first met the Reverend on the top of Box Hill one Saturday afternoon. Bike had punctured, and the Reverend gave me the loan of his cyclists' repairing outfit. We had our tea together. Watercress, bread-and-butter, and two sorts of jam—one bob per head. He issued an invite to his diggings in the Temple. Cocoa and cigs. of an evening. Regular pally, him and me was. Then he got into the way of taking me down to a Boys' Club that he had started. Terrors they were, so to put it. Fair out-and-out terrors. But they all thought a lot of the Reverend, and so did I. Consequently it was all right. The next link in the chain was a chap called Cloyster. James Orlebar Cloyster. The Reverend brought him down to teach boxing. For my own part, I don't fancy anything in the way of brutality. The club, so I thought, had got on very nicely with more intellectual pursuits: draughts, chess, bagatelle, and what-not. But the Rev. wanted boxing, and boxing it had to be. Not that it would have done for him or me to have mixed ourselves up in it. He had his congregation to consider, and I am often on duty at the downstairs counter before the very heart of the public. A black eye or a missing tooth wouldn't have done at all for either of us, being, as we were, in a sense, officials. But Cloy-

ster never seemed to realise this. Not to put too fine a
point upon it, Cloyster was not my idea of a gentleman.
He had no tact.

The next link was a confirmed dipsomaniac. A terrible phrase. Unavoidable, though. A very evil man is
Tom Blake. Yet out of evil cometh good, and it was
Tom Blake, who, indirectly, stopped the boxing lessons. The club boys never wore the gloves after
drunken Blake's visit.

I shall never—no, positively never forget that night
in June when matters came to a head in Shaftesbury
Avenue. Oh, I say, it was a bit hot—very warm.

Each successive phase is limned indelibly—that's the
sort of literary style I've got, if wanted—on the tablets
of my memory.

I'd been up West, and who should I run across in
Oxford Street but my old friend, Charlie Cookson.
Very good company is Charlie Cookson. See him at a
shilling hop at the Holborn: he's pretty much all there
all the time. Well-known follower—of course, purely as
an amateur—of the late Dan Leno, king of comedians;
good penetrating voice; writes his own in-between
bits—you know what I mean: the funny observations
on mothers-in-law, motors, and marriage, marked
"Spoken" in the song-books. Fellows often tell him he'd
make a mint of money in the halls, and there's a rumour flying round among us who knew him in the
"Moon" that he was seen coming out of a Bedford
Street Variety Agency the other day.

Well, I met Charlie at something after ten. Directly
he spotted me he was at his antics, standing stock still
on the pavement in a crouching attitude, and grasping
his umbrella like a tomahawk. His humour's always
high-class, but he's the sort of fellow who doesn't care a
blow what he does. Chronic in that respect, absolutely.
The passers-by couldn't think what he was up to.

"Whoop—whoop—whoop!" that's what he said. He did, straight. Only *yelled* it. I thought it was going a bit too far in a public place. So, to show him, I just said "Good evening, Cookson; how are you this evening?" With all his entertaining ways he's sometimes slow at taking a hint. No tact, if you see what I mean.

In this case, for instance, he answered at the top of his voice: "Bolly Golly, yah!" and pretended to scalp me with his umbrella. I immediately ducked, and somehow knocked my bowler against his elbow. He caught it as it was falling off my head. Then he said, "Indian brave give little pale face chief his hat." This was really too much, and I felt relieved when a police-man told us to move on. Charlie said: "Come and have two penn'orth of something."

Well, we stayed chatting over our drinks (in fact, I was well into my second lemon and dash) at the Stock-wood Hotel until nearly eleven. At five to, Charlie said good-bye, because he was living in, and I walked out into the Charing Cross Road, meaning to turn down Shaftesbury Avenue so as to get a breath of fresh air. Outside the Oxford there was a bit of a crowd. I asked a man standing outside a tobacconist's what the trouble was. "Says he won't go away without kissing the girl that sang 'Empire Boys,'" was the reply. "Bin shiftin' it, 'e 'as, not 'arf!" Sure enough, from the midst of the crowd came:

> Yew are ther boys of the Empire,
>   Steady an' brave an' trew.
> Yew are the wuns
> She calls 'er sons
>   An' I luv yew.

I had gone, out of curiosity, to the outskirts of the crowd, and before I knew what had happened I found myself close to the centre of it. A large man in dirty corduroys stood with his back to me. His shape seemed strangely familiar. Still singing, and swaying to horrible angles all over the shop, he slowly pivoted round. In a moment I recognised the bleary features of Tom Blake. At the same time he recognised me. He stretched out a long arm and seized me by the shoulder. "Oh," he sobbed, "I thought I 'ad no friend in the wide world except 'er; but now I've got yew it's orlright. Yus, yus, it's orlright." A murmur, almost a cheer it was, circulated among the crowd. But a policeman stepped up to me.

"Now then," said the policeman, "wot's all this about?"

> Yew are the wuns
> She calls 'er sons—

shouted Blake.

"Ho, that's yer little game, is it?" said the policeman. "Move on, d'yer hear? Pop off."

"I will," said Blake. "I'll never do it again. I promise faithful never to do it again. I've found a fren'."

"Do you know this covey?" asked the policeman.

"Deny it, if yer dare," said Blake. "Jus' you deny it, that's orl, an' I'll tell the parson."

"Slightly, constable," I said. "I mean, I've seen him before."

"Then you'd better take 'im off if you don't want 'im locked up."

" 'Im want me locked up? We're bosum fren's, ain't we, old dear?" said Blake, linking his arm in mine and dragging me away with him. Behind us, the policeman was shunting the spectators. Oh, it was excessively displeasing to any man of culture, I can assure you.

How we got along Shaftesbury I don't know. It's a subject I do not care to think about.

By leaning heavily on my shoulder and using me, so to speak, as ballast, drunken Blake just managed to make progress, I cannot say unostentatiously, but at any rate not so noticeably as to be taken into custody.

I didn't know, mind you, where we were going to, and I didn't know when we were going to stop.

In this frightful manner of progression we had actually gained sight of Piccadilly Circus when all of a sudden a voice hissed in my ear: "Sidney Price, I am disappointed in you." Hissed, mind you. I tell you, I jumped. Thought I'd bitten my tongue off at first.

If drunken Blake hadn't been clutching me so tight you could have knocked me down with a feather: bowled me over clean. It startled Blake a goodish bit, too. All along the Avenue he'd been making just a quiet sort of snivelling noise. Crikey, if he didn't speak up quite perky. "O, my fren'," he says. "So drunk and yet so young." Meaning me, if you please.

It was too thick.

"You blighter," I says. "You *blooming* blighter. You talk to me like that. Let go of my arm and see me knock you down."

I must have been a bit excited, you see, to say that. Then I looked round to see who the other individual was. You'll hardly credit me when I tell you it was the Reverend. But it was. Honest truth, it was the Rev. John Hatton and no error. His face fairly frightened me. Simply blazing: red: fair scarlet. He kept by the side of us and let me have it all he could. "I thought you knew better, Price," that's what he said. "I thought you knew better. Here are you, a friend of mine, a member of the Club, a man I've trusted, going about the streets of London in a bestial state of disgusting intoxication. That's enough in itself. But you've done worse than that. You've lured poor Blake into intemperance. Yes, with all your advantages of education and up-bringing, you deliberately set to work to put temptation in the way of poor, weak, hard-working Blake. Drunkenness is Blake's besetting sin, and you——"

Blake had been silently wagging his head, as pleased as Punch at being called hardworking. But here he shoved in his oar.

" 'Ow dare yer!" he burst out. "I ain't never tasted a drop o' beer in my natural. Born an' bred teetotal, that's wot I was, and don't yew forget it, neither."

"Blake," said the Reverend, "that's not the truth."

"Call me a drunkard, do yer?" replied Blake. "Go on. Say it again. Say I'm a blarsted liar, won't yer? Orlright, then I shall run away."

And with that he wrenched himself away from me and set off towards the Circus. He was trying to run, but his advance took the form of semi-circular sweeps all over the pavement. He had circled off so unexpectedly that he had gained some fifty yards before we realised what was happening. "We must stop him," said the Reverend.

"As I'm intoxicated," I said, coldly (being a bit fed up with things), "I should recommend you stopping him, Mr. Hatton."

"I've done you an injustice," said the Reverend.

"You have," said I.

Blake was now nearing a policeman. "Stop him!" we both shouted, starting to run forward.

The policeman brought Blake to a standstill.

"Friend of yours?" said the constable when we got up to him.

"Yes," said the Reverend.

"You ought to look after him better," said the constable.

"Well, really, I like that!" said the Reverend; but he caught my eye and began laughing. "Our best plan," he said, "is to get a four-wheeler and go down to the Temple. There's some supper there. What do you say?"

"I'm on," I said, and to the Temple we accordingly journeyed.

Tom Blake was sleepy and immobile. We spread him without hindrance on a sofa, where he snored peacefully whilst the Reverend brought eggs and a slab of bacon out of a cupboard in the kitchen. He also brought a frying-pan, and a bowl of fat.

"Is your cooking anything extra good?" he asked.

"No, Mr. Hatton," I answered, rather stiff; "I've never cooked anything in my life." I may not be in a very high position in the "Moon," but I've never descended to menial's work yet.

For about five minutes after that the Reverend was too busy to speak. Then he said, without turning his head away from the hissing pan, "I wish you'd do me a favour, Price."

"Certainly," I said.

"Look in the cupboard and see whether there are any knives, forks, plates, and a loaf and a bit of butter, will you?"

I looked, and, sure enough, they were there.

"Yes, they're all here," I called to him.

"And is there a tray?"

"Yes, there's a tray."

"Now, it's a funny thing that my laundress," he shouted back, "can't bring in breakfast things for more than one on that particular tray. She's always complaining it's too small, and says I ought to buy a bigger one."

"Nonsense," I exclaimed, "she's quite wrong about that. You watch what I can carry in one load." And I packed the tray with everything he had mentioned.

"What price that?" I said, putting the whole boiling on the sitting-room table.

The Reverend began to roar with laughter. "It's ridiculous," he chuckled. "I shall tell her it's ridiculous. She ought to be ashamed of herself."

Shortly after we had supper, previously having aroused Blake.

The drunken fellow seemed completely restored by his repose. He ate more than his share of the eggs and bacon, and drank five cups of tea. Then he stretched himself, lit a clay pipe, and offered us his tobacco box, from which the Reverend filled his briar. I remained true to my packet of "Queen of the Harem." I shall think twice before chucking up cig. smoking as long as "Queen of the Harem" don't go above tuppence-half-penny per ten.

We were sitting there smoking in front of the fire—it was a shade parky for the time of year—and not talking a great deal, when the Reverend said to Blake, "Things are looking up on the canal, aren't they, Tom?"

"No," said Blake; "things ain't lookin' up on the canal."

"Got a little house property," said the Reverend, "to spend when you feel like it?"

"No," said the other; "I ain't got no 'ouse property to spend."

"Ah," said the Reverend, cheesing it, and sucking his pipe.

"Dessay yer think I'm free with the rhino?" said Blake after a while.

"I was only wondering," said the Reverend.

Blake stared first at the Reverend and then at me.

"Ever remember a party of the name of Cloyster, Mr. James Orlebar Cloyster?" he inquired.

"Yes," we both said.

" 'E's a good man," said Blake.

"Been giving you money?" asked the Reverend.

"'E's put me into the way of earning it. It's the sorfest job ever I struck. 'E told me not to say nothin', and I said as 'ow I wouldn't. But it ain't fair to Mr. Cloyster, not keeping of it dark ain't. Yew don't know what a noble 'eart that man's got, an' if you weren't fren' of 'is I couldn't have told you. But as you are fren's of 'is, as we're all fren's of 'is, I'll take it on myself to tell you wot that noble-natured man is giving me money for. Blowed if 'e shall 'ide his bloomin' light under a blanky bushel any longer." And then he explained that for putting his name to a sheet or two of paper, and addressing a few envelopes, he was getting more money than he knew what to do with. "Mind you," he said, "I play it fair. I only take wot he says I'm to take. The rest goes to 'im. My old missus sees to all that part of it 'cos she's quicker at figures nor wot I am."

While he was speaking, I could hardly contain myself. The Reverend was listening so carefully to every word that I kept myself from interrupting; but when he'd got it off his chest, I clutched the Reverend's arm, and said, "What's it mean?"

"Can't say," said he, knitting his brows.

"Is he straight?" I said, all on the jump.

"I hope so."

"'Hope so.' You don't think there's a doubt of it?"

"I suppose not. But surely it's very unselfish of you to be so concerned over Blake's business."

"Blake's business be jiggered," I said. "It's my business, too. I'm doing for Mister James Orlebar Cloyster exactly what Blake's doing. And I'm making money. You don't understand."

"On the contrary, I'm just beginning to understand. You see, I'm doing for Mr. James Orlebar Cloyster exactly the same service as you and Blake. And I'm getting money from him, too."

Chapter 18

ONE IN THE EYE

(Sidney Price's narrative continued)

"Serpose I oughtn't ter 'ave let on, that's it, ain't it?" from Tom Blake.

"Seemed to me that if one of the three gave the show away to the other two, the compact made by each of the other two came to an end automatically," from myself.

"The reason I have broken my promise of secrecy is this: that I'm determined we three shall make a united demand for a higher rate of payment. You, of course, have your own uses for the money. I need mine for those humanitarian objects for which my whole life is lived," from the Reverend.

"Wot 'o," said Blake. "More coin. Wot 'o. Might 'ave thought o' that before."

"I'm with you, sir," said I. "We're entitled to a higher rate, I'll make a memo to that effect."

"No, no," said the Reverend. "We can do better than that. We three should have a personal interview with Cloyster and tell him our decision."

"When?" I asked.

"Now. At once. We are here together, and I see no

reason to prevent our arranging the matter within the hour."

"But he'll be asleep," I objected.

"He won't be asleep much longer."

"Yus, roust 'im outer bed. That's wot I say. Wot 'o for more coin."

It was now half-past two in the morning. I'd missed the 12:15 back to Brixton slap bang pop hours ago, so I thought I might just as well make a night of it. We jumped into our overcoats and hats, and hurried to Fleet Street. We walked towards the Strand until we found a four-wheeler. We then drove to No. 23, Walpole Street.

The clocks struck three as the Reverend paid the cab.

"Hullo!" said he. "Why, there's a light in Cloyster's sitting-room. He can't have gone to bed yet. His late hours save us a great deal of trouble." And he went up the two or three steps which led to the front door.

A glance at Tom Blake showed me that the barge-driver was alarmed. He looked solemn and did not speak. I felt funny, too. Like when I first handed round the collection-plate in our parish church. Sort of empty feeling.

But the Reverend was all there, spry and business-like.

He leaned over the area railing and gave three short, sharp taps on the ground floor window with his walking-stick.

Behind the lighted blind appeared the shadow of a man's figure.

"It's he!" "It's him!" came respectively and simultaneously from the Reverend and myself.

After a bit of waiting the latch clicked and the door opened. The door was opened by Mr. Cloyster himself. He was in evening dress and hysterics. I thought I had

heard a rummy sound from the other side of the door.
Couldn't account for it at the time. Must have been
him laughing.

At the sight of us he tried to pull himself together.
He half succeeded after a bit, and asked us to come in.

To say his room was plainly furnished doesn't
express it. The apartment was like a prison cell. I've
never been in gaol, of course. But I read "Convict 99"
when it ran in a serial. The fire was out, the chairs
were hard, and the whole thing was uncomfortable.
Never struck such a shoddy place in my natural, ever
since I called on a man I know slightly who was in
"The Hand of Blood" travelling company No. 3 B.

"Delighted to see you, I'm sure," said Mr. Cloyster.
"In fact, I was just going to sit down and write to you."

"Really," said the Reverend. "Well, we've come of
our own accord, and we've come to talk business."
Then turning to Blake and me he added, "May I state
our case?"

"Most certainly, sir," I answered. And Blake gave a
nod.

"Briefly, then," said the Reverend, "our mission is
this: that we three want our contracts revised."

"What contracts?" said Mr. Cloyster.

"Our contracts connected with your manuscripts."

"Since when have the several matters of business
which I arranged privately with each of you become
public?"

"Tonight. It was quite unavoidable. We met by
chance. We are not to blame. Tom Blake was——"

"Yes, he looks as if he had been."

"Our amended offer is half profits."

"More coin," murmured Blake huskily. "Wot 'o!"

"I regret that you've had your journey for nothing."

"You refuse?"

"Absolutely."

"My dear Cloyster, I had expected you to take this attitude; but surely it's childish of you. You are bound to accede. Why not do so at once?"

"Bound to accede? I don't follow you."

"Yes, bound. The present system which you are working is one you cannot afford to destroy. That is clear, because, had it not been so, you would never have initiated it. I do not know for what reason you were forced to employ this system, but I do know that powerful circumstances must have compelled you to do so. You are entirely in our hands."

"I said just now I was delighted to see you, and that I had intended to ask you to come to me. One by one, of course; for I had no idea that the promise of secrecy which you gave me had been broken."

The Reverend shrugged his shoulders.

"Do you know why I wanted to see you?"

"No."

"To tell you that I had decided to abandon my system. To notify you that you would, in future, receive no more of my work."

There was a dead silence.

"I think I'll go home to bed," said the Reverend.

Blake and myself followed him out.

Mr. Cloyster thanked us all warmly for the excellent way in which we had helped him. He said that he was now engaged to be married, and had to save every penny. "Otherwise, I should have tried to meet you in this affair of the half-profits." He added that we had omitted to congratulate him on his engagement.

His words came faintly to our ears as we tramped down Walpole Street; nor did we, as far as I can remember, give back any direct reply.

Tell you what it was just like. Reminded me of it

even at the time: that picture of Napoleon coming back from Moscow. The Reverend was Napoleon, and we were the generals; and if there were three humpier men walking the streets of London at that moment I should have liked to have seen them.

Chapter 19

IN THE SOUP

(Sidney Price's narrative continued)

They give you a small bonus at the "Moon" if you get through a quarter without being late, which just shows the sort of scale on which the "Moon" does things. Cookson, down at the Oxford Street Emporium, gets fined regular when he's late. Shilling the first hour and twopence every five minutes after. I've known gentlemen in banks, railway companies, dry goods, and woollen offices, the Indian trade, jute, tea— every manner of shop—but they all say the same thing, "We are ruled by fear." It's fear that drags them out of bed in the morning; it's fear that makes them bolt, or even miss, their sausages; it's fear that makes them run to catch their train. But the "Moon's" method is of a different standard. The "Moon" does not intimidate; no, it entwines itself round, it insinuates itself into, the hearts of its employees. It suggests, in fact, that we should not be late by offering us this small bonus. No insurance office and, up to the time of writing, no other assurance office has been able to boast as much. The same cause is at the bottom of the "Moon's" high reputation, both inside and outside. It does things in a big way. It's spacious.

The "Moon's" timing system is great, too. Great in its simplicity. The regulation says you've got to be in the office by ten o'clock. Suppose you arrive with ten minutes to spare. You go into the outer office (there's only one entrance—the big one in Threadneedle Street) and find on the right-hand side of the circular counter a ledger. The ledger is open: there is blotting-paper and a quill pen beside it. Everyone's name is written in alphabetical order on the one side of the ledger and on the other side there is a blank page ruled down the middle with a red line. Having made your appearance at ten to ten, you put your initials in a line with your name on the page opposite and to the left of the division. If, on the other hand, you've missed your train, and don't turn up till ten minutes *past* ten, you've got to initial your name on the other side of the red line. In the space on the right of the line, a thick black dash has been drawn by Leach, the cashier. He does this on the last stroke of ten. It makes the page look neat, he says. Which is quite right and proper. I see his point of view entirely. The ledger must look decent in an office like the "Moon." Tommy Milner agrees with me. He says that not only does it look better, but it prevents unfortunate mistakes on the part of those who come in late. They might forget and initial the wrong side.

After ten the book goes into Mr. Leach's private partition, and you've got to go in there to sign.

It was there when I came into the office on the morning after we'd been to talk business with Mr. Cloyster. It had been there about an hour and a half.

"Lost your bonus, Price, my boy," said genial Mr. Leach. And the General Manager, Mr. Fennell, who had stepped out of his own room close by, heard him say it.

"I do not imagine that Mr. Price is greatly perturbed on that account. He will, no doubt, shortly be forsaking

us for literature. What Commerce loses, Art gains,"
said the G.M.

He may have meant to be funny, or he may not.
Some of those standing near took him one way, others
the other. Some gravely bowed their heads, others
burst into guffaws. The G.M. often puzzled his staff in
that way. All were anxious to do the right thing by him,
but he made it so difficult to tell what the right thing
was.

But, as I went down the basement stairs to change
my coat in the clerks' locker-room, I understood from
the G.M.'s words how humiliating my position was.

I had always been a booky sort of person. At home it
had been a standing joke that, when a boy, I would
sooner spend a penny on *Tit-Bits* than liquorice. And it
was true. Not that I disliked liquorice. I liked *Tit-Bits*
better, though. So the thing had gone on. I advanced
from *Deadwood Dick* to Hall Caine and Guy Boothby;
and since I had joined the "Moon" I had actually gone
a buster and bought *Omar Khayyam* in the Golden Trea-
sury series. Added to which, I had recently composed a
little lyric for a singer at the "Moon's" annual smoking
concert. The lines were topical and were descriptive of
our Complete Compensation Policy. Tommy Milner
was the vocalist. He sang my composition to a hymn
tune. The refrain went:

> Come and buy a C.C.Pee-ee!
> If you want immunitee-ee
> From the accidents which come
> Please plank down your premium.
> Life is diff'rent, you'll agree
> *Repeat* When you've got a C.C.P.

The Throne Room of the Holborn fairly rocked with
applause.

Well, it was shortly afterwards that I had received a visit from Mr. Cloyster—the visit which ended in my agreeing to sign whatever manuscripts he sent me, and forward him all cheques for a consideration of ten per cent. Softest job ever a man had. Easy money. Kudos— I had almost too much of it. Which takes me back to the G.M.'s remark about my leaving the office. Since he's bought that big house at Regent's Park he's done a lot of entertaining at the restaurants. His name's always cropping up in the "Here and There" column, and naturally he's a subscriber to the *Strawberry Leaf.* The G.M. has everything of the best and plenty of it. (You don't see the G.M. with memo. forms tucked round his cuffs: he wears a clean shirt every morning of his life. All tip-top people have their little eccentricities.) And the *Strawberry Leaf,* the smartest, goeyest, personalest weekly, is never missing from his drawing-room what-not. Every week it's there, regular as clockwork. That's what started my literary reputation among the fellows at the "Moon." Mr. Cloyster was contributing a series of short dialogues to the *Strawberry Leaf*—called, "In Town." These, on publication, bore my own signature. As a matter of fact, I happened to see the G.M. showing the first of the series to Mr. Leach in his private room. I've kept it by me, and I don't wonder the news created a bit of a furore. This was it:—

IN TOWN
BY SIDNEY PRICE

No. I.—THE SECRECY OF THE BALLET

(You are standing under the shelter of the Criterion's awning. It is 12.30 of a summer's morning. It is pouring in torrents. A quick and sudden rain storm. It won't last long, and it doesn't mean any harm. But what's sport to it is death to you. You were touring the Circus in a new hat. Brand new.

Couldn't spot your tame cabby. Hadn't a token. Spied the Cri's awning. Dashed at it. But it leaks. Not so much as the sky though. Just enough, however, to do your hat no good. You mention this to Friendly Creature with umbrella, and hint that you would like to share that weapon.)

FRIENDLY CREATURE. Can't give you all, boysie. Mine's new, too.

YOU (*in your charming way*). Well, of course. You wouldn't be a woman if you hadn't a new hat.

FRIENDLY CREATURE. Do women always have new hats?

YOU (*edging under the umbrella*). Women have new hats. New women have hats.

FRIENDLY CREATURE. Don't call me a woman, ducky; I'm a lady.

YOU. I must be careful. If I don't flatter you, you'll take your umbrella away.

FRIENDLY CREATURE (*changing subject*). There's Matilda.

YOU. Where?

FRIENDLY CREATURE. Coming towards us in that landaulette.

YOU. Looks fit, doesn't she?

FRIENDLY CREATURE. Her! She's a blooming rotter.

YOU. Not so loud. She'll hear you.

FRIENDLY CREATURE (*raising her voice*). Good job. I want her to. *Stumer!*

YOU. S-s-s-sh! What *are* you saying? Matilda's a duchess now.

FRIENDLY CREATURE. I know.

YOU. But you mustn't say "Stumer" to a duchess unless——

FRIENDLY CREATURE. Well?

YOU. Unless you're a duchess yourself?

FRIENDLY CREATURE. I am. At least I was. Only I chucked it.

You. But you said you were a lady.

Friendly Creature. So I am. An extra lady—front row, second O.P.

You. How rude of me. Of course you were a duchess. I know you perfectly. Gorell Barnes said——

Friendly Creature. Drop it. What's the good of the secrecy of the ballet if people are going to remember every single thing about you?

(At this point the rain stops. By an adroit flanking movement you get away without having to buy her a lunch.)

Everyone congratulated me. "Always knew he had it in him," "Found his vocation," "A distinctly clever head," "Reaping in the shekels"—that was the worst part. The "Moon," to a man, was bent on finding out "how much Sidney Price makes out of his bits in the papers." Some dropped hints—the G.M., Leach, and the men at the counter. Others, like Tommy Milner, asked slap out. You may be sure I didn't tell them a fixed sum. But it was hopeless to say I was getting the small sum which my ten per cent. commission worked out at. On the other hand, I dared not pretend I was being paid at the usual rates. I should have gone broke in twenty-four hours. You have no idea how constantly I was given the opportunity of lending five shillings to important members of the "Moon" staff. It struck me then—and I have found out for certain since—that there is a popular anxiety to borrow from a man who earns money by writing. The earnings of a successful writer are, to the common intelligence, something he ought not really to have. And anyone, in default of abstracting his income, may fall back upon taking up his time.

It did, no doubt, appear that I was coining the ready. Besides the *Strawberry Leaf, Features,* and *The Key of the*

Street were printing my signed contributions in weekly series. *The Mayfair*, too, had announced on its placards, "A Story in Dialogue, by Sidney Price."

This, then, was my position on the morning when I was late at the "Moon" and lost my bonus.

Whilst I went up in the lift to the New Business Room, and whilst I was entering the names and addresses of inquirers in the Proposal Book, I was trying to gather courage to meet what was in store.

For the future held this: that my name would disappear from the papers as suddenly as it had arrived there. People would want to know why I had given up writing. "Written himself out," "No staying power," "As short-lived as a Barnum monstrosity": these would be the remarks which would herald ridicule and possibly pity.

And I should be in just the same beastly fix at the "Hollyhocks" as I was at the "Moon." What would my people say? What would Norah say?

There was another reason, too, why a stoppage of the ten per cent. cheques would be a whack in the eye. You see, I had been doing myself well on them—uncommonly well. I had ordered, as a present to my parents, new furniture for the drawing-room. I had pressed my father to have a small greenhouse put up at my expense. He had always wanted one, but had never been able to run to it. And I had taken Norah about a good deal. Our weekly visit to a matinée (upper circle and ices), followed by tea at the Cabin or Lyons' Popular, had become an institution. We had gone occasionally to a ball at the Town Hall.

What would Norah say when all this ended abruptly without any explanation?

There was no getting away from it. Sidney Price was in the soup.

Chapter 20

NORAH WINS HOME
(Sidney Price's narrative continued)

My signed work had run out. For two weeks nothing had been printed over my signature. So far no comment had been raised. But it was only a question of days. But then one afternoon it all came right. It was like this.

I was sitting eating my lunch at Eliza's in Birchin Lane. Twenty minutes was the official allowance for the meal, and I took my twenty minutes at two o'clock. The *St. Stephen's Gazette* was lying near me. I picked it up. Anything to distract my thoughts from the trouble to come. That was how I felt. Reading mechanically the front page, I saw a poem, and started violently. This was the poem:—

A CRY
Hands at the tiller to steer:
A star in the murky sky:
Water and waste of mere:
Whither and why?

Sting of absorbent night:
Journey of weal or woe:
And overhead the light:
We go—we go?

156

Darkness a mortal's part,
  Mortals of whom we are:
Come to a mortal's heart,
  Immortal star.

Thos. Blake.

June 6th.

"Rummy, very rummy," I exclaimed. The poem was dated yesterday. Had Mr. Cloyster, then, continued to work his system with Thomas Blake to the exclusion of the Reverend and myself?

Still worrying over the thing, I turned over the pages of the paper until I chanced to see the following paragraph:

LITERARY GOSSIP

Few will be surprised to learn that the Rev. John Hatton intends to publish another novel in the immediate future. Mr. Hatton's first book, *When It Was Lurid,* created little less than a furore. The work on which he is now engaged, which will bear the title of *The Browns of Brixton,* is a tender sketch of English domesticity. This new vein of Mr. Hatton's will, doubtless, be distinguished by the naturalness of dialogue and sanity of characterisation of his first novel. Messrs. Prodder and Way are to publish it in the autumn.

"He's running the Reverend again, is he?" said I to myself. "And I'm the only one left out. It's a bit thick."

That night I wrote to Blake and to the Reverend asking whether they had been taken on afresh, and if so, couldn't I get a look in, as things were pretty serious.

The Reverend's reply arrived first:

THE TEMPLE,
June 7th.

Dear Price,—

As you have seen, I am hard at work at my new novel. The leisure of a novelist is so scanty that I

know you'll forgive my writing only a line. I am in
no way associated with James Orlebar Cloyster, nor
do I wish to be. Rather I would forget his very existence.

You are aware of the interests which I have at
heart: social reform, the education of the sub-
merged, the physical needs of the young—there is
no necessity for me to enumerate my ideals further.
To get quick returns from philanthropy, to put re-
medial organisation into speedy working order
wants capital. Cloyster's system was one way of ob-
taining some of it, but when that failed I had to
look out for another. I'm glad I helped in the system, for it made me realise how large an income a
novelist can obtain. I'm glad it failed because its failure suggested that I should try to get for myself
those vast sums which I had been getting for the
selfish purse of an already wealthy man. Unconsciously, he has played into my hands. I read his
books before I signed them, and I find that I have
thoroughly absorbed those tricks of his, of style and
construction, which opened the public's coffers to
him. *The Browns of Brixton* will eclipse anything that
Cloyster has previously done, for this reason, that it
will out-Cloyster Cloyster. It is Cloyster with im-
provements.

In thus abducting his novel-reading public I shall
feel no compunction. His serious verse and his society dialogues bring him in so much that he cannot
be in danger of financial embarrassment.

Yours sincerely, John Hatton.

Now this letter set my brain buzzing like the engine
of a stationary Vanguard. I, too, had been in the habit
of reading Mr. Cloyster's dialogues before I signed and
sent them off. I had often thought to myself, also, that
they couldn't take much writing, that it was all a knack;
and the more I read of them the more transparent the

knack appeared to me to be. Just for a lark, I sat down that very evening and had a go at one. Taking the Park for my scene, I made two or three theatrical celebrities whose names I had seen in the newspapers talk about a horse race. At least, one talked about a horse race, and the others thought she was gassing about a new musical comedy, the name of the play being the same as the name of the horse, "The Oriental Belle." A very amusing muddle, with lots of *doubles entendres,* and heaps of adverbial explanation in small print. Such as:

Miss Adeline Genée
(with the faint, incipient blush which Mrs. Adair uses
to test her Rouge Imperial).

That sort of thing.

I had it typed, and I said, "Price, my boy, there's more Mr. Cloyster in this than ever Mr. Cloyster could have put into it." And the editor of the *Strawberry Leaf* printed it next issue as a matter of course. I say, "as a matter of course" with intention, because the fellows at the "Moon" took it as a matter of course, too. You see, when it first appeared, I left the copy about the desk in the New Business Room, hoping Tommy Milner or some of them would rush up and congratulate me. But they didn't. They simply said, "Don't litter the place up, old man. Keep your papers, if you *must* bring 'em here, in your locker downstairs." One of them *did* say, I fancy, something about its "not being quite up to my usual." They didn't know it was my maiden effort at original composition, and I couldn't tell them. It was galling, you'll admit.

However, I quickly forgot my own troubles in wondering what Mr. Cloyster was doing. No editor, I foresaw, would accept his society stuff as long as mine was in the market. They wouldn't pay for Cloyster whilst they were offered the refusal of super-Cloyster. Wasn't likely. You must understand I wasn't over-easy in my conscience about the affair. I had, in a manner of speaking, pinched Mr. Cloyster's job. But then, I argued to myself, he was earning quite as much as was good for any one man by his serious verse.

And at that very minute our slavey, little Ethelbertina, knocked at my bedroom door and gave me a postcard. It was addressed to me in thick, straggly writing, and was so covered with thumb-marks that a Bertillon expert would have gone straight off his nut at the sight of it. "My usbend," began the postcard, "as received yourn. E as no truk wif the other man E is a pots imself an e can do a job of potry as orfen as e 'as a mine to your obegent servent Ada Blake. P.S. me an is ole ant do is writin up for im."

So then I saw how that "Cry" thing in the *St. Stephen's* had come there.

*   *   *   *   *

You heard me give my opinion about telling Norah my past life. Well, you'll agree with me now that there's practically nothing to tell her.

There *is,* of course, little Miss Richards, the waitress in the smoking-room of the Piccadilly Cabin. Her, I mean, with the fuzzy golden hair done low. You've often exchanged "Good evening" with her, I'm sure. Her hair's done low: she used to make rather a point of telling me that. Why, I don't know, especially as it was always tidy and well off her shoulders.

And then there was the haughty lady who sold programmes in the Haymarket Amphitheatre—but she's got the sack, so Cookson informs me.

Therefore, as I shall tell Norah plainly that I disapprove of the Cabin, the past can hatch no egg of discord in the shape of the Cast-Off Glove.

The only thing that I can think of as needing suppression is the part I played in Mr. Cloyster's system.

There's no doubt that the Reverend, Blake and I have, between us, put a fairly considerable spoke in Mr. Cloyster's literary wheel. But what am I to do? To begin with, it's no use my telling Norah about the affair, because it would do her no good, and might tend possibly to lessen her valuation of my capabilities. At present, my dialogues dazzle her; and once your *fiancée* is dazzled the basis of matrimonial happiness is assured. Again, looking at it from Mr. Cloyster's point of view, what good would it be to him if I were to stop writing? Both the editor and the public have realised by now that his work is only second-rate. He can never hope to get a tenth of his original prices, even if his work is accepted, which it won't be; for directly I leave his market clear, someone else will collar it slap off.

Besides, I've no right to stop my dialogues. My duty to Norah is greater than my duty to Mr. Cloyster. Unless I continue to be paid by literature I shall not be able to marry Norah until three years next quarter. The "Moon" has passed a rule about it, and an official who marries on an income not larger than eighty pounds per annum is liable to dismissal without notice.

Norah's mother wouldn't let her wait three years, and though fellows have been known to have had a couple of kids at the time of their official marriage, I personally couldn't stand the wear and tear of that hole-and-corner business. It couldn't be done.

(End of Sidney Price's narrative.)

Julian Eversleigh's
Narrative

Chapter 21

THE TRANSPOSITION OF SENTIMENT

It is all very, very queer. I do not understand it at all. It makes me sleepy to think about it.

A month ago I hated Eva. Tomorrow I marry her by special licence.

Now, what *about* this?

My brain is not working properly. I am becoming jerky.

I tried to work the thing out algebraically. I wrote it down as an equation, thus:—

$$
\begin{array}{rcl}
\text{HATRED, denoted by} & x + \text{Eva.} \\
\text{REVERSE OF HATRED,} \quad " \quad \quad " & y + \text{Eva} \\
\text{ONE MONTH} \quad " \quad \quad " & z.
\end{array}
$$

From which we get:—
$$x + \text{Eva} = (y + \text{Eva})z.$$

And if anybody can tell me what that means (if it means anything—which I doubt) I shall be grateful. As I said before, my brain is not working properly.

There is no doubt that my temperament has changed, and in a very short space of time. A month ago I was soured, cynical, I didn't brush my hair, and I slept too much. I talked a good deal about Life. Now I am blithe and optimistic. I use pomade, part in the middle, and sleep eight hours and no more. I have not made an epigram for days. It is all very queer.

I took a new attitude towards life at about a quarter to three on the morning after the Gunton-Cresswells's dance. I had waited for James in his rooms. He had been to the dance.

Examine me for a moment as I wait there.

I had been James' friend for more than two years and a half. I had watched his career from the start. I knew him before he had located exactly the short cut to Fortune. Our friendship embraced the whole period of his sudden, extraordinary success.

Had not envy by that time been dead in me, it might have been pain to me to watch him accomplish unswervingly with his effortless genius the things I had once dreamt I, too, would laboriously achieve.

But I grudged him nothing. Rather, I had pleasure in those triumphs of my friend.

There was no confidence we had withheld from one another.

When he told me of his relations with Margaret Goodwin he had counted on my sympathy as naturally as he had requested and received my advice.

To no living soul, save James, would I have confessed my own tragedy—my hopeless love for Eva.

It is inconceivable that I should have misjudged a man so utterly as I misjudged James.

That is the latent factor at the root of my problem. The innate rottenness, the cardiac villainy of James Orlebar Cloyster.

In a measure it was my own hand that laid the train which eventually blew James' hidden smoulder of fire into the blazing beacon of wickedness, in which my friend's Satanic soul is visible in all its lurid nakedness.

I remember well that evening, mild with the prelude of spring, when I evolved for James' benefit the System. It was a device which was to preserve my friend's liberty and, at the same time, to preserve my friend's honour. How perfect in its irony!

Margaret Goodwin, mark you, was not to know he could afford to marry her, and my system was an instrument to hide from her the truth.

He employed that system. It gave him the holiday he asked for. He went into Society.

Among his acquaintances were the Gunton-Cresswells, and at their house he met Eva. Whether his determination to treat Eva as he had treated Margaret came to him instantly, or by degrees I do not know. Inwardly he may have had his scheme matured in embryo, but outwardly he was still the accomplished hypocrite. He was the soul of honour—outwardly. He was the essence of sympathetic tact as far as his specious exterior went. Then came the 27th of May. On that date the first of James Orlebar Cloyster's masks was removed.

I had breakfasted earlier than usual, so that by the time I had walked from Rupert Court to Walpole Street it was not yet four o'clock.

James was out. I thought I would wait for him. I stood at his window. Then I saw Margaret Goodwin. What features! What a complexion! "And James," I murmured, "is actually giving this the miss in baulk!" I discovered, at that instant, that I did not know James. He was a fool.

In a few hours I was to discover he was a villain, too.

She came in and I introduced myself to her. I almost forget what pretext I manufactured, but I remember I

persuaded her to go back to Guernsey that very day. I
think I said that James was spending Friday till Monday in the country, and had left no address. I was determined that they should not meet. She was far too
good for a man who obviously did not appreciate her
in the least.

We had a very pleasant chat. She was charming. At
first she was apt to touch on James a shade too
frequently, but before long I succeeded in diverting
our conversation into less uninteresting topics.

She talked of Guernsey, I of London. I said I felt I
had known her all my life. She said that one had, un-
deniably, one's affinities.

I said, "Might I think of her as 'Margaret'?"

She said it was rather unconventional, but that she
could not control my thoughts.

I said, "There you are wrong—Margaret."

She said, "Oh, what are you saying, Mr. Eversleigh?"

I said I was thinking out loud.

On the doorstep she said, "Well, yes—Julian—you
may write to me—sometimes. But I won't promise to
answer."

Angel!

The next thing that awakened me was the coming of
James.

After I had given him a suitable version of
Margaret's visit, he told me he was engaged to Eva.
That was an astounding thing; but what was more astounding was that James had somehow got wind of the
real spirit of my interview with Margaret.

I have called James Orlebar Cloyster a fool: I have
called him a villain. I will never cease to call him a genius. For by some marvellous capacity for introspec-
tion, by some incredible projection of his own mind
into other people's matters, he was able to tax me to

my face with an attempt to win his former *fiancée's* af-
fections. I tried to choke him off. I used every ounce of
bluff I possessed. In vain. I left Walpole Street in a
state approaching mental revolution.

My exact feelings towards James were too intricate to
be defined in a single word. Not so my feelings towards
Eva. "Hate" supplied the lacuna in her case.

Thus the month began.

The next point of importance is my interview with
Mrs. Gunton-Cresswell. She had known all along how
matters stood in regard to Eva and myself. She had not
been hostile to me on that account. She had only
pointed out that as I could do nothing towards supporting Eva I had better keep away when my cousin
was in London. That was many years ago. Since then
we had seldom met. Latterly, not at all. Invitations still
arrived from her, but her afternoon parties clashed
with my after-breakfast pipe, and as for her evening
receptions—well, by the time I had pieced together the
various component parts of my dress clothes, I found
myself ready for bed. That is to say, more ready for
bed than I usually am.

I went to Mrs. Gunton-Cresswell in a very bitter
mood. I was bent on trouble.

"I've come to congratulate Eva," I said.

Mrs. Gunton-Cresswell sighed.

"I was afraid of this," she said.

"The announcement was the more pleasant," I went
on, "because James has been a bosom friend of mine."

"I'm afraid you are going to be extremely disagreeable about your cousin's engagement," she said.

"I am," I answered her. "Very disagreeable. I intend
to shadow the young couple, to be constantly meeting
them, calling attention to them. James will most likely
have to try to assault me. That may mean a black eye

for dear James. It will certainly mean the police court. Their engagement will be, in short, a succession of hideous *contretemps,* a series of laughable scenes."

"Julian," said Mrs. Gunton-Cresswell, "hitherto you have acted manfully toward Eva. You have been brave. Have you no regard for Eva?"

"None," I said.

"Nor for Mr. Cloyster?"

"Not a scrap."

"But why are you behaving in this appallingly selfish way?"

This was a facer. I couldn't quite explain to her how things really were, so I said:

"Never you mind. Selfish or not, Mrs. Gunton-Cresswell, I'm out for trouble."

That night I had a letter from her. She said that in order to avoid all unpleasantness, Eva's engagement would be of the briefest nature possible. That the marriage was fixed for the twelfth of next month; that the wedding would be a very quiet one; and that until the day of the wedding Eva would not be in London.

It amused me to find how thoroughly I had terrified Mrs. Gunton-Cresswell. How excellently I must have acted, for, of course, I had not meant a word I had said to that good lady.

In the days preceding the twelfth of June I confess I rather softened to James. The *entente cordiale* was established between us. He told me how irresistible Eva had been that night; mentioned how completely she had carried him away. Had she not carried me away in precisely the same manner once upon a time?

He swore he loved her as dearly as—— (I can't call to mind the simile he employed, though it was masterly and impressive.) I even hinted that the threats I had used in the presence of Mrs. Gunton-Cresswell were not serious. He thanked me, but said I had frightened her to such good purpose that the date would now have to stand. "You will not be surprised to hear," he added, "that I have called in all my work. I shall want every penny I make. The expenses of an engaged man are hair-raising. I send her a lot of flowers every morning—you've no conception how much a few orchids cost. Then, whenever I go to see her I take her some little present—a gold-mounted umbrella, a bicycle lamp, or a patent scent-bottle. I'm indebted to you, Julian, positively indebted to you for cutting short our engagement."

I now go on to point two: the morning of the twelfth of June.

Hurried footsteps on my staircase. A loud tapping at my door. The church clock chiming twelve. The agitated, weeping figure of Mrs. Gunton-Cresswell approaching my hammock. A telegram thrust into my hand. Mrs. Gunton-Cresswell's hysterical exclamation, "You infamous monster—you—you are at the bottom of this."

All very disconcerting. All, fortunately, very unusual.

My eyes were leaden with slumber, but I forced myself to decipher the following message, which had been telegraphed to West Kensington Lane:

Wedding must be postponed.—CLOYSTER.

"I've had no hand in this," I cried; "but," I added enthusiastically, "it serves Eva jolly well right."

Chapter 22

A CHAT WITH JAMES
(*Julian Eversleigh's narrative continued*)

Mrs. Gunton-Cresswell seemed somehow to drift away after that. Apparently I went to sleep again, and she didn't wait.

When I woke, it was getting on for two o'clock. I breakfasted, with that magnificent telegram propped up against the teapot; had a bath, dressed, and shortly before five was well on my way to Walpole Street.

The more I thought over the thing, the more it puzzled me. Why had James done this? Why should he wish to treat Eva in this manner? I was delighted that he had done so, but why had he? A very unexpected person, James.

James was lying back in his shabby old armchair, smoking a pipe. There was tea on the table. The room seemed more dishevelled than ever. It would have been difficult to say which presented the sorrier spectacle, the room or its owner.

He looked up as I came in, and nodded listlessly. I poured myself out a cup of tea, and took a muffin. Both were cold and clammy. I went to the bell.

"What are you doing?" asked James.

"Only going to ring for some more tea," I said.

"No, don't do that. I'll go down and ask for it. You don't mind using my cup, do you?"

He went out of the room, and reappeared with a jug of hot water.

"You see," he explained, "if Mrs. Blankley brings in another cup she'll charge for two teas instead of one."

"It didn't occur to me," I said. "Sorry."

"It sounds mean," mumbled James.

"Not at all," I said. "You're quite right not to plunge into reckless extravagance."

James blushed slightly—a feat of which I was surprised to see that he was capable.

"The fact is——" he began.

I interrupted him.

"Never mind about that," I said. "What I want to know is—what's the meaning of this?" And I shoved the bilious-hued telegraph form under his nose, just as Mrs. Gunton-Cresswell had shoved it under mine.

"It means that I'm done," he said.

"I don't understand."

"I'll explain. I have postponed my marriage for the same reason that I refused you a clean cup—because I cannot afford luxuries."

"It may be my dulness; but, still, I don't follow you. What exactly are you driving at?"

"I'm done for. I'm on the rocks. I'm a pauper."

"A what?"

"A pauper."

I laughed. The man was splendid. There was no other word for it.

"And shall I tell you something else that you are?" I said. "You are a low, sneaking liar. You are playing it low down on Eva."

He laughed this time. It irritated me unspeakably.

"Don't try to work off the hollow, mirthless laugh

dodge on me," I said, "because it won't do. You're a blackguard, and you know it."

"I tell you I'm done for. I've barely a penny in the world."

"Rot!" I said. "Don't try that on me. You've let Eva down plop, and I'm jolly glad; but all the same you're a skunk. Nothing can alter that. Why don't you marry the girl?"

"I can't," he said. "It would be too dishonourable."

"Dishonourable?"

"Yes. I haven't got enough money. I couldn't ask her to share my poverty with me. I love her too dearly."

I was nearly sick. The beast spoke in a sort of hushed, soft-music voice as if he were the self-sacrificing hero in a melodrama. The stained-glass expression on his face made me feel homicidal.

"Oh, drop it," I said. "Poverty! Good Lord! Isn't two thousand a year enough to start on?"

"But I haven't got two thousand a year."

"Oh, I don't pretend to give the figures to a shilling."

"You don't understand. All I have to live on is my holiday work at the *Orb*."

"What!"

"Oh, yes; and I'm doing some lyrics for Briggs for the second edition of *The Belle of Wells*. That'll keep me going for a bit, but it's absolutely out of the question to think of marrying anyone. If I can keep my own head above water till the next vacancy occurs at the *Orb* I shall be lucky."

"You're mad."

"I'm not, though I dare say I shall be soon, if this sort of thing goes on."

"I tell you you are mad. Otherwise you'd have called in your work, and saved yourself having to pay those commissions to Hatton and the others. As it is, I believe they've somehow done you out of your cheques, and the shock of it has affected your brain."

"My dear Julian, it's a good suggestion, that about calling in my work. But it comes a little late. I called it in weeks ago."

My irritation increased.

"What is the use of lying like that?" I said angrily. "You don't seem to credit me with any sense at all. Do you think I never read the papers and magazines? You can't have called in your work. The stuff's still being printed over the signatures of Sidney Price, Tom Blake, and the Rev. John Hatton."

I caught sight of a *Strawberry Leaf* lying on the floor beside his chair. I picked it up.

"Here you are," I said. "Page 324. Short story. 'Lady Mary's Mistake,' by Sidney Price. How about that?"

"That's it, Julian," he said dismally; "that's just it. Those three devils have pinched my job. They've learned the trick of the thing through reading my stuff, and now they're turning it out for themselves. They've cut me out. My market's gone. The editors and publishers won't look at me. I have had eleven printed rejection forms this week. One editor wrote and said that he did not want John-Hatton-and-water. That's why I sent the wire."

"Let's see those rejection forms."

"You can't. They're burnt. They got on my nerves, and I burnt them."

"Oh," I said, "they're burnt, are they?"

He got up, and began to pace the room.

"But I shan't give up, Julian," he cried, with a sickening return of the melodrama hero manner; "I shan't give up. I shall still persevere. The fight will be terrible. Often I shall feel on the point of despair. Yet I shall win through. I feel it, Julian. I have the grit in me to do it. And meanwhile"—he lowered his voice, and seemed surprised that the orchestra did not strike up the slow music—"meanwhile, I shall ask Eva to wait."

To wait! The colossal, the Napoleonic impudence of the man! I have known men who seemed literally to exude gall, but never one so overflowing with it as James Orlebar Cloyster. As I looked at him standing there and uttering that great speech, I admired him. I ceased to wonder at his success in life.

I shook my head.

"I can't do it," I said regretfully. "I simply cannot begin to say what I think of you. The English language isn't equal to it. I cannot, off-hand, coin a new phraseology to meet the situation. All I can say is that you are unique."

"What do you mean?"

"Absolutely unique. Though I had hoped you would have known me better than to believe that I would swallow the ludicrous yarn you've prepared. Don't you ever stop and ask yourself on these occasions if it's good enough?"

"You don't believe me!"

"My dear James!" I protested. "Believe you!"

"I swear it's all true. Every word of it."

"You seem to forget that I've been behind the scenes. I'm not simply an ordinary member of the audience. I know how the illusion is produced. I've seen the strings pulled. Why, dash it, *I* showed you how to pull them. I never came across a finer example of seething the kid in its mother's milk. I put you up to the system, and you turn round and try to take me in with it. Yes, you're a wonder, James."

"You don't mean to say you think——!"

"Don't be an ass, James. Of course I do. You've had the brazen audacity to attempt to work off on Eva the game you played on Margaret. But you've made a mistake. You've forgotten to count me."

I paused, and ate a muffin. James watched me with fascinated eyes.

"You," I resumed, "ethically, I despise. Eva, personally, I detest. It seems, therefore, that I may expect to extract a certain amount of amusement from the situation. The fun will be inaugurated by your telling Eva that she may have to wait five years. You will state, also, the amount of your present income."

"Suppose I decline?"

"You won't."

"You think not?"

"I am sure."

"What would you do if I declined?"

"I should call upon Mrs. Gunton-Cresswell and give her a quarter of an hour's entertainment by telling her of the System, and explaining to her, in detail, the exact method of its working and the reason why you set it going. Having amused Mrs. Gunton-Cresswell in this manner, I should make similar revelations to Eva. It would not be pleasant for you subsequently, I suppose, but we all have our troubles. That would be yours."

He hesitated.

"As if they'd believe it," he said, weakly.

"I think they would."

"They'd laugh at you. They'd think you were mad."

"Not when I produced John Hatton, Sidney Price, and Tom Blake in a solid phalanx, and asked them to corroborate me."

"They wouldn't do it," he said, snatching at a straw. "They wouldn't give themselves away."

"Hatton might hesitate to, but Tom Blake would do it like a shot."

As I did not know Tom Blake, a moment's reflection might have told James that this was bluff. But I had gathered a certain knowledge of the bargee's character from James's conversation, and I knew that he was a drunken, indiscreet sort of person who might be expected to reveal everything in circumstances such as I had described; so I risked the shot, and it went home. James's opposition collapsed.

"I shall then," administering the *coup de grâce*, "arrange a meeting between the Gunton-Cresswells and old Mrs. Goodwin."

"Thank you," said James, "but don't bother. On second thoughts I will tell Eva about my income and the five years' wait."

"Thanks," I said; "it's very good of you. Good-bye."

And I retired, chuckling, to Rupert Street.

Chapter 23

IN A HANSOM

(Julian Eversleigh's narrative continued)

I spent a pleasant week in my hammock awaiting developments.

At the end of the week came a letter from Eva. She wrote:—

> *My Dear Julian,*—You haven't been to see us for ages. Is Kensington Lane beyond the pale?
> *Your affectionate cousin,*
>
> *Eva.*

"You vixen," I thought. "Yes; I'll come and see you fast enough. It will give me the greatest pleasure to see you crushed and humiliated."

I collected my evening clothes from a man of the name of Attenborough, whom I employ to take care of them when they are not likely to be wanted; found a white shirt, which looked presentable after a little pruning of the cuffs with a razor; and drove to the Gunton-Cresswells's in time for dinner.

There was a certain atmosphere of unrest about the house. I attributed this at first to the effects of the James Orlebar Cloyster bomb-shell, but discovered that

179

it was in reality due to the fact that Eva was going out to a fancy-dress ball that night.

She was having dinner sent up to her room, they told me, and would be down presently. There was a good deal of flitting about going on. Maids on mysterious errands shot up and down stairs. Old Mr. Gunton-Cresswell, looking rather wry, was taking cover in his study when I arrived. Mrs. Gunton-Cresswell was in the drawing-room.

Before Eva came down I got a word alone with her. "I've had a nice, straight-forward letter from James," she said, "and he has done all he can to put things straight with us."

"Ah!" said I.

"That telegram, he tells me, was the outcome of a sudden panic."

"Dear me!" I said.

"It seems that he made some most ghastly mistake about his finances. What exactly happened I can't quite understand, but the gist of it is, he thought he was quite well off, whereas, really, his income is infinitesimal."

"How odd!" I remarked.

"It sounds odd; in fact, I could scarcely believe it until I got his letter of explanation. I'll show it to you. Here it is."

I read James Orlebar Cloyster's letter with care. It was not particularly long, but I wish I had a copy of it; for it is the finest work in an imaginative vein that has ever been penned.

"Masterly!" I exclaimed involuntarily.

"Yes, isn't it?" she echoed. "Enables one to grasp thoroughly how the mistake managed to occur."

"Has Eva seen it?"

"Yes."

"I notice he mentions five years as being about the period——"

"Yes; it's rather a long engagement, but, of course, she'll wait, she loves him so."

Eva now entered the room. When I caught sight of her I remembered I had pictured her crushed and humiliated. I had expected to gloat over a certain dew-iness of her eyes, a patient drooping of her lips. I will say plainly there was nothing of that kind about Eva to-night.

She had decided to go to the ball as Peter Pan.

The costume had rather scandalised old Mr. Gunton-Cressell, a venerable Tory who rarely spoke except to grumble. Even Mrs. Gunton-Cresswell, who had lately been elected to the newly-formed *Les Serfs d'Avenir,* was inclined to deprecate it.

But I was sure Eva had chosen the better part. The dress suited her to perfection. Her legs are the legs of a boy.

As I looked at her with concentrated hatred, I real-ised I had never seen a human soul so radiant, so brimming with *espièglerie,* so altogether to be desired.

"Why, Julian, is it you. This *is* good of you!"

It was evident that the past was to be waived. I took my cue.

"Thanks, Eva," I said; "it suits you admirably."

Events at this point move quickly.

Another card of invitation is produced. Would I care to use it, and take Eva to the ball?

"But I'm not in fancy dress."

Overruled. Fancy dress not an essential. Crowds of men there in ordinary evening clothes.

So we drove off.

We hardly exchanged a syllable. No one has much to say just before a dance.

I looked at Eva out of the corner of my eye, trying to discover just what it was in her that attracted men. I knew her charm, though I flattered myself that I was proof against it. I wanted to analyse it.

Her photograph is on the table before me as I write. I look at it critically. She is not what I should describe as exactly a type of English beauty. You know the sort of beauty I mean? Queenly, statuesque, a daughter of the gods, divinely fair. Her charm is not in her features. It is in her expression.

Tonight, for instance, as we drove to the ball, there sparkled in her eyes a light such as I had never seen in them before. Every girl is animated at a ball, but this was more than mere animation. There was a latent devilry about her; and behind the sparkle and the glitter a film, a mist, as it were, which lent almost a pathos to her appearance. The effect it had on me was to make me tend to forget that I hated her.

We arrive. I mutter something about having the pleasure.

Eva says I can have the last two waltzes.

Here comes a hiatus. I am told that I was seen dancing, was observed to eat an excellent supper, and was noticed in the smoking-room with a cigarette in my mouth.

At last the first of my two waltzes. The Eton Boating Song—one of my favourites. I threaded my way through the room in search of her. She was in neither of the doorways. I cast my eyes about the room. Her costume was so distinctive that I could hardly fail to see her.

I did see her.

She was dancing my waltz with another man.

The thing seemed to numb my faculties. I stood in the doorway, gaping. I couldn't understand it. The illogical nature of my position did not strike me. It did not occur to me that as I hated the girl so much, it was much the best thing that could happen that I should see as little of her as possible. My hatred was entirely concentrated on the bounder who had stolen my dance. He was a small, pink-faced little beast, and it maddened me to see that he danced better than I could ever have done.

As they whirled past me she smiled at him.

I rushed to the smoking-room.

Whether she gave my other waltz to the same man, or whether she chose some other partner, or sat alone waiting for me, I do not know. When I returned to the ballroom the last waltz was over, and the orchestra was beginning softly to play the first extra. It was *"Tout Passe,"* an air that has always had the power to thrill me.

My heart gave a bound. Standing in the doorway just in front of me was Eva.

I drew back.

Two or three men came up, and asked her for the dance. She sent them away, and my heart leaped as they went.

She was standing with her back towards me. Now she turned. Our eyes met. We stood for a moment looking at one another.

Then I heard her give a little sigh; and instantly I forgot everything—my hatred, my two lost dances, the pink-faced blighter—everything. Everything but that I loved her.

"Tired, Eva?" I said.

"Perhaps I am," she replied. "Yes, I am, Julian."

"Give me this one," I whispered. "We'll sit it out."

"Very well. It's so hot in here. We'll go and sit it out in a hansom, shall we? I'll get my cloak."

I waited, numbed by her absence. Her cloak was pale pink. We walked out together into the starry night. A few yards off stood a hansom. "Drive to the corner of Sloane Street," I said to the man, "by way of the Park."

The night was very still.

I have said that I had forgotten everything except that I loved her. Could I remember now? Now, as we drove together through the empty streets alone, her warm, palpitating body touching mine.

James, and his awful predicament, which would last till Eva gave him up; Eva's callous treatment of my former love for her; my own newly-acquired affection for Margaret; my self-respect—these things had become suddenly of no account.

"Eva," I murmured; and I took her hand.

"Eva . . ."

Her wonderful eyes met mine. The mist in them seemed to turn to dew. "My darling," she whispered, very low.

The road was deserted. We were alone.

I drew her face to mine and kissed her.

* * * * *

My love for her grows daily.

Old Gunton-Cresswell has introduced me to a big firm of linoleum manufacturers. I am taking over their huge system of advertising next week. My salary will be enormous. It almost frightens me. Old Mr. Cresswell tells me that he had had the job in his mind for me for some time, and had, indeed, mentioned to his wife and Eva at lunch that day that he intended to write to me about it. I am more grateful to him than I can ever make him understand. Eva, I know, cares nothing for money—she told me so—but it is a comfort to feel that I can keep her almost in luxury.

I have given up my rooms in Rupert Street.

I sleep in a bed.

I do Sandow exercises.

I am always down to breakfast at eight-thirty sharp.
I smoke less.
I am the happiest man on earth.

(End of Julian Eversleigh's narrative.)

Narrative Resumed
by James Orlebar Cloyster

Chapter 24

A RIFT IN THE CLOUDS

O perfidy of woman! O feminine inconstancy! That is the only allusion I shall permit to escape me on the subject of Eva Eversleigh's engagement to that scoundrel Julian.

I had the news by telegraph, and the heavens darkened above me, whilst the solid earth rocked below.

I had been trapped into dishonour, and even the bait had been withheld from me.

But it was not the loss of Eva that troubled me most. It should have outweighed all my other misfortunes and made them seem of no account, but it did not. Man is essentially a materialist. The prospect of an empty stomach is more serious to him than a broken heart. A broken heart is the luxury of the well-to-do. What troubled me more than all other things at this juncture was the thought that I was face to face with starvation, and that only the grimmest of fights could enable me to avoid it. I quaked at the prospect. The early struggles of the writer to keep his head above water form an experience which does not bear repetition. The hopeless feeling of chipping a little niche for oneself out of the solid rock with a nib is a nightmare even in times of prosperity. I remembered the grey days of my literary apprenticeship, and I shivered at the thought that I must go through them again.

I examined my position dispassionately over a cup of coffee at Groom's, in Fleet Street. Groom's was a recognised *Orb rendezvous*. When I was doing "On Your Way," one or two of us used to go down Fleet Street for coffee after the morning's work with the regularity of machines. It formed a recognised break in the day.

I thought things over. How did I stand? Holiday work at the *Orb* would begin very shortly, so that I should get a good start in my race. Fermin would be going away in a few weeks, then Gresham, and after that Fane, the man who did the "People and Things" column. With luck I ought to get a clear fifteen weeks of regular work. It would just save me. In fifteen weeks I ought to have got going again. The difficulty was that I had dropped out. Editors had forgotten my work. John Hatton they knew, and Sidney Price they knew; but who was James Orlebar Cloyster? There would be much creaking of joints and wobbling of wheels before my triumphal car could gather speed again. But, with a regular salary coming in week by week from the *Orb,* I could endure this. I became almost cheerful. It is an exhilarating sensation having one's back against the wall.

Then there was Briggs, the actor. The very thought of him was a tonic. A born fighter, with the energy of six men, he was an ideal model for me. If I could work with a sixth of his dash and pluck, I should be safe. He was giving me work. He might give me more. The new edition of the *Belle of Wells* was due in another fortnight. My lyrics would be used, and I should get paid for them. Add this to my *Orb* salary, and I should be a man of substance.

I glared over my coffee-cup at an imaginary John Hatton.

"You thought you'd done me, did you?" I said to him. "By Gad! I'll have the laugh of you all yet."

I was shaking my fist at him when the door opened. I hurriedly tilted back my chair, and looked out of the window.

"Hullo, Cloyster."

I looked round. It was Fermin. Just the man I wanted to see.

He seemed depressed. Even embarrassed.

"How's the column?" I asked.

"Oh, all right," he said awkwardly. "I wanted to see you about that. I was going to write to you."

"Oh, yes," I said, "of course. About the holiday work. When are you off?"

"I was thinking of starting next week."

"Good. Sorry to lose you, of course, but——"

He shuffled his feet.

"You're doing pretty well now at the game, aren't you, Cloyster?" he said.

It was not to my interests to cry myself down, so I said that I was doing quite decently. He seemed relieved.

"You're making quite a good income, I suppose? I mean, no difficulty about placing your stuff?"

"Editors squeal for it."

"Because, otherwise what I wanted to say to you might have been something of a blow. But it won't affect you much if you're doing plenty of work elsewhere."

A cold hand seemed laid upon my heart. My mind leaped to what he meant. Something had gone wrong with the *Orb* holiday work, my sheet-anchor.

"Do you remember writing a par about Stickney, the

butter-scotch man, you know, ragging him when he got his peerage?"

"Yes."

It was one of the best paragraphs I had ever done. A two-line thing, full of point and sting. I had been editing "On Your Way" that day, Fermin being on a holiday and Gresham ill; and I had put the paragraph conspicuously at the top of the column.

"Well," said Fermin, "I'm afraid there was rather trouble about it. Hamilton came into our room yesterday, and asked if I should be seeing you. I said I thought I should. 'Well, tell him,' said Hamilton, 'that that paragraph of his about Stickney has only cost us five hundred pounds. That's all.' And he went out again. Apparently Stickney was on the point of advertising largely with the *Orb,* and had backed out in a huff. Today, I went to see him about my holiday, and he wanted to know who was coming in to do my work. I mentioned you, and he absolutely refused to have you in. I'm awfully sorry about it."

I was silent. The shock was too great. Instead of drifting easily into my struggle on a comfortable weekly salary, I should have to start the tooth-and-nail fighting at once. I wanted to get away somewhere by myself, and grapple with the position.

I said good-bye to Fermin, retaining sufficient presence of mind to treat the thing lightly, and walked swiftly along the restless Strand, marvelling at what I had suffered at the hands of Fortune. The deceiver of Margaret, deceived by Eva, a pauper! I covered the distance between Groom's and Walpole Street in sombre meditation.

In a sort of dull panic I sat down immediately on my arrival, and tried to work. I told myself that I must turn out something, that it would be madness to waste a moment.

I sat and chewed my pen from two o'clock till five, but not a page of printable stuff could I turn out. Looking back at myself at that moment, I am not surprised that my ideas did not flow. It would have been a wonderful triumph of strength of mind if I had been able to write after all that had happened. Dr. Johnson has laid it down that a man can write at any time, if he sets himself to it earnestly; but mine were exceptional circumstances. My life's happiness and my means for supporting life at all, happy or otherwise, had been swept away in a single morning; and I found myself utterly unable to pen a coherent sentence.

At five o'clock I gave up the struggle, and rang for tea.

While I was having tea there was a ring at the bell, and my landlady brought in a large parcel.

I recognised the writing on the label. The hand was Margaret's. I wondered in an impersonal sort of way what Margaret could be sending to me. From the feel of it the contents were paper.

It amuses me now to think that it was a good half-hour before I took the trouble to cut the string. Fortune and happiness were waiting for me in that parcel, and I would not bother to open it. I sat in my chair, smoking and thinking, and occasionally cast a gloomy eye at the parcel. But I did not open it. Then my pipe went out, and I found that I had no matches in my pocket. There were some at the farther end of the mantelpiece. I had to get up to reach them, and, once up, I found myself filled with a sufficient amount of energy to take a knife from the table and cut the string.

Languidly I undid the brown paper. The contents were a pile of typewritten pages and a letter.

It was the letter over which my glassy eyes travelled first.

"My own dear, brave, old darling James," it began, and its purport was that she had written a play, and wished me to put my name to it and hawk it round: to pass off as my work her own amateurish effort at playwriting. Ludicrous. And so immoral, too. I had always imagined that Margaret had a perfectly flawless sense of honesty. Yet here she was asking me deliberately to impose on the credulity of some poor, trusting theatrical manager. The dreadful disillusionment of it shocked me.

Most men would have salved their wounded susceptibilities by putting a match to the manuscript without further thought or investigation.

But I have ever been haunted by a somewhat over-strict conscience, and I sat down there and then to read the stupid stuff.

At seven o'clock I was still reading.

My dinner was brought in. I bolted it with Margaret's play propped up against the potato dish.

I read on and on. I could not leave it. Incredible as it would appear from anyone but me, I solemnly assure you that the typewritten nonsense I read that evening was nothing else than *The Girl who Waited*.

Chapter 25

BRIGGS TO THE RESCUE
(*James Orlebar Cloyster's narrative continued*)

I finished the last page, and I laid down the typescript reverently. The thing amazed me. Unable as I was to turn out a good acting play of my own, I was, nevertheless, sufficiently gifted with an appreciation of the dramatic to be able to recognise such a play when I saw it. There were situations in Margaret's comedy which would grip a London audience, and force laughter and tears from it. . . . Well, the public side of that idiotic play is history. Everyone knows how many nights it ran, and the Press from time to time tells its readers what were the profits from it that accrued to the author.

I turned to Margaret's letter and re-read the last page. She put the thing very well, very sensibly. As I read, my scruples began to vanish. After all, was it so very immoral, this little deception that she proposed?

"I have written down the words," she said; "but the conception is yours. The play was inspired by you. But for you I should never have begun it." Well, if she put it like that——

"You alone are able to manage the business side of the production. You know the right men to go to. To

195

approach them on behalf of a stranger's work is far less likely to lead to success."

(True, true.)

"I have assumed, you will see, that the play is certain to be produced. But that will only be so if you adopt it as your own."

(There was sense in this.)

"Claim the authorship, and all will be well."

"I will," I said.

I packed up the play in its brown paper, and rushed from the house. At the post-office, at the bottom of the King's Road, I stopped to send a telegram. It consisted of the words, "Accept thankfully.—Cloyster."

Then I took a cab from the rank at Sloane Square, and told the man to drive to the stage-door of the Briggs Theatre in Shaftesbury Avenue.

The cab-rank in Sloane Square is really a Home for Superannuated Horses. It is a sort of equine Athenæum. No horse is ever seen there till it has passed well into the sere and yellow. A Sloane Square cab-horse may be distinguished by the dignity of its movements. It is happiest when walking.

The animal which had the privilege of making history by conveying me and *The Girl who Waited* to the Briggs Theatre was asthmatic, and, I think, sickening for the botts. I had plenty of time to cool my brain and think out a plan of campaign.

Stanley Briggs, whom I proposed to try first, was the one man I should have liked to see in the part of James, the hero of the piece. The part might have been written round him.

There was the objection, of course, that *The Girl who Waited* was not a musical comedy, but I knew he would consider a straight play, and put it on if it suited him. I was confident that *The Girl who Waited* would be just what he wanted.

The problem was how to get him to himself for a sufficient space of time. When a man is doing the work of half a dozen he is likely to get on in the world, but he has, as a rule, little leisure for conversation.

My octogenarian came to a standstill at last at the stage-door, and seemed relieved at having won safely through a strenuous bit of work.

I went through in search of my man.

His dressing-room was the first place I drew. I knew that he was not due on the stage for another ten minutes. Mr. Richard Belsey, his valet, was tidying up the room as I entered.

"Mr. Briggs anywhere about, Richard?" I asked.

"Down on the side, sir, I think. There's a new song in tonight for Mrs. Briggs, and he's gone to listen how it goes."

"Which side, do you know?"

"O.P., sir, I think."

I went downstairs and through the folding-doors into the wings. The O.P. corner was packed—standing room only—and the overflow reached nearly to the doors. The Black Hole of Calcutta was roomy compared with the wings on the night of a new song. Everybody who had the least excuse for being out of his or her dressing-room at that moment was peering through odd chinks in the scenery. Chorus-girls, show-girls, chorus-men, principals, children, scene-shifters, and other theatrical *fauna* waited in a solid mass for the arrival of the music-cue.

The atmosphere behind the scenes has always had the effect of making me feel as if my boots were number fourteens and my hands, if anything, larger. Directly I have passed the swing-doors I shuffle like one oppressed with a guilty conscience. Outside I may have been composed, even jaunty. Inside I am hangdog. Beads of perspiration form on my brow. My collar tightens. My boots begin to squeak. I smile vacuously.

I shuffled, smiling vacuously and clutching the type-script of *The Girl who Waited,* to the O.P. corner. I caught the eye of a tall lady in salmon-pink, and said "Good evening" huskily—my voice is always husky behind the scenes: elsewhere it is like some beautiful bell. A piercing whisper of "Sh-h-h-!" came from somewhere close at hand. This sort of thing does not help bright and sparkling conversation. I sh-h-hed, and passed on.

At the back of the O.P. corner Timothy Prince, the comedian, was filling in the time before the next entrance by waltzing with one of the stage-carpenters. He suspended the operation to greet me.

"Hullo, dear heart," he said, "how goes it?"

"Seen Briggs anywhere?" I asked.

"Round on the prompt side, I think. He was here a second ago, but he dashed off."

At this moment the music-cue was given, and a considerable section of the multitude passed on to the stage.

Locomotion being rendered easier, I hurried round to the prompt side.

But when I arrived there were no signs of the missing man.

"Seen Mr. Briggs anywhere?" I asked.

"Here a moment ago," said one of the carpenters. "He went out after Miss Lewin's song began. I think he's gone round the other side."

I dashed round to the O.P. corner again. He had just left.

Taking up the trail, I went to his dressing-room once more.

"You're just too late, sir," said Richard; "he was here a moment ago."

I decided to wait.

"I wonder if he'll be back soon."

"He's probably downstairs. His call is in another two minutes."

I went downstairs, and waited on the prompt side. Sir Boyle Roche's bird was sedentary compared with this elusive man.

Presently he appeared.

"Hullo, dear old boy," he said. "Welcome to Elsmore. Come and see me before you go, will you? I've got an idea for a song."

"I say," I said, as he flitted past, "can I——"

"Tell me later on."

And he sprang on to the stage.

By the time I had worked my way, at the end of the performance, through the crowd of visitors who were waiting to see him in his dressing-room, I found that he had just three minutes in which to get to the Savoy to keep an urgent appointment. He explained that he was just dashing off. "I shall be at the theatre all to-morrow morning, though," he said. "Come round about twelve, will you?"

There was a rehearsal at half-past eleven next morning. When I got to the theatre I found him on the stage. He was superintending the chorus, talking to one man about a song and to two others about motors, and dictating letters to his secretary. Taking advantage of this spell of comparative idleness, I advanced (l.c.) with the typescript.

"Hullo, old boy," he said, "just a minute! Sit down, won't you? Have a cigar."

I sat down on the Act One sofa, and he resumed his conversations.

"You see, laddie," he said, "what you want in a song like this is tune. It's no good doing stuff that your wife

and family and your aunts say is better than Wagner.
They don't want that sort of thing here—Dears, we
simply can't get on if you won't do what you're told.
Begin going off while you're singing the last line of the
refrain, not after you've finished. All back. I've told
you a hundred times. Do try and get it right—I simply
daren't look at a motor bill. These fellers at the garage
cram it on—I mean, what can you *do?* You're up
against it—Miss Hinckel, I've got seventy-five letters I
want you to take down. Ready? 'Mrs. Robert Boodle,
Sandringham, Mafeking Road, Balham. Dear Madam:
Mr. Briggs desires me to say that he fears that he has
no part to offer to your son. He is glad that he made
such a success at his school theatricals.' 'James Winter-
botham, Pleasant Cottage, Rhodesia Terrace, Stock-
well. Dear Sir: Mr. Briggs desires me to say that he
remembers meeting your wife's cousin at the public
dinner you mention, but that he fears he has no part at
present to offer to your daughter.' 'Arnold H. Bodgett,
Wistaria Lodge . . .' "

My attention wandered.

At the end of a quarter of an hour he was ready
for me.

"I wish you'd have a shot at it, old boy," he said, as
he finished sketching out the idea for the lyric, "and let
me have it as soon as you can. I want it to go in at the
beginning of the second act. Hullo, what's that you're
nursing?"

"It's a play. I was wondering if you would mind
glancing at it if you have time?"

"Yours?"

"Yes. There's a part in it that would just suit you."

"What is it? Musical comedy?"

"No. Ordinary comedy."

"I shouldn't mind putting on a comedy soon. I must
have a look at it. Come and have a bit of lunch."

One of the firemen came up, carrying a card.

"Hullo, what's this? Oh, confound the feller! He's always coming here. Look here: tell him that I'm just gone out to lunch, but can see him at three. Come along, old boy."

He began to read the play over the coffee and cigars. He read it straight through, as I had done.

"What rot!" he said, as he turned the last page.

"Isn't it!" I exclaimed enthusiastically. "But won't it go?"

"Go?" he shouted, with such energy that several lunchers spun round in their chairs, and a Rand magnate, who was eating peas at the next table, started and cut his mouth. "Go? It's the limit! This is just the sort of thing to get right at them. It'll hit them where they live. What made you think of that drivel at the end of Act Two?"

"Genius, I suppose. What do you think of James as a part for you?"

"Top hole. Good Lord, I haven't congratulated you! Consider it done."

"Thanks."

We drained our liqueur glasses to *The Girl who Waited* and to ourselves.

Briggs, after a lifetime spent in doing three things at once, is not a man who lets a great deal of grass grow under his feet. Before I left him that night the "ideal cast" of the play had been jotted down, and much of the actual cast settled. Rehearsals were in full swing within a week, and the play was produced within ten days of the demise of its predecessor.

Meanwhile, the satisfactory sum which I received in advance of royalties was sufficient to remove any regrets as to the loss of the *Orb* holiday work. With *The Girl who Waited* in active rehearsal, "On Your Way" lost in importance.

Chapter 26

MY TRIUMPH

(James Orlebar Cloyster's narrative continued)

O n the morning of the day for which the production had been fixed, it dawned upon me that I
had to meet Mrs. Goodwin and Margaret at Waterloo.
All through the busy days of rehearsal, even on those
awful days when everything went wrong and actresses,
breaking down, sobbed in the wings and refused to be
comforted, I had dimly recognised the fact that when I
met Margaret I should have to be honest with her.
Plans for evasion had been half-matured by my inven-
tive faculties, only to be discarded, unpolished, on account of the insistent claims of the endless rehearsals.
To have concocted a story with which to persuade
Margaret that I stood to lose money if the play succeeded would have been a clear day's work. And I had
no clear days.

But this was not all. There was another reason.
Somehow my sentiments with regard to her were
changing again. It was as if I were awaking from some
dream. I felt as if my eyes had been blindfolded to
prevent me seeing Margaret as she really was, and that
now the bandage had been removed. As the day of
production drew nearer, and the play began to take

shape, I caught myself sincerely admiring the girl who could hit off, first shot, the exact shade of drivel which the London stage required. What culture, what excessive brain-power she must have. How absurdly *naïve*, how impossibly melodramatic, how maudlinly sentimental, how improbable—in fact, how altogether womanly she must have grown.

Womanly! That did it. I felt that she was womanly. And it came about that it was my Margaret of the Cobo shrimping journeys that I was prepared to welcome as I drove that morning to Waterloo Station.

And so, when the train rolled in, and the Goodwins alighted, and Margaret kissed me, by an extraordinarily lucky chance I found that I loved her more dearly than ever.

That *première* is still fresh in my memory.

Mrs. Goodwin, Margaret, and myself occupied the stage box, and in various parts of the house I could see the familiar faces of those whom I had invited as my guests.

I felt it was the supreme event of my life. It was *the* moment. And surely I should have spoilt it all unless my old-time friends had been sitting near me.

Eva and Julian were with Mr. and Mrs. Gunton-Cresswell in the box opposite us. To the Barrel Club I had sent the first row of the dress circle. It was expensive, but worth it. Hatton and Sidney Price were in the stalls. Tom Blake had preferred a free pass to the gallery. Kit and Malim were at the back of the upper circle (this was, Malim told me, Kit's own choice).

One by one the members of the orchestra took their places for the overture, and it was to the appropriate strains of "Land of Hope and Glory" that the curtain rose on the first act of my play.

The first act, I should mention (though it is no doubt

superfluous to do so) is bright and suggestive, but ends
on a clear, firm note of pathos. That is why, as soon as
the lights went up, I levelled my glasses at the eyes of
the critics. Certainly in two cases, and, I think, in a
third, I caught the glint of tear-drops. One critic was
blowing his nose, another sobbed like a child, and I
had a hurried vision of a third staggering out to the
foyer with his hand to his eyes. Margaret was removing
her own tears with a handkerchief. Mrs. Goodwin's un-
moved face may have hidden a lacerated soul, but she
did not betray herself. Hers may have been the
thoughts that lie too deep for tears. At any rate, she
did not weep. Instead, she drew from her reticule the
fragmentary writings of an early Portuguese author.
These she perused during the present and succeeding
entr'actes.

Pressing Margaret's hand, I walked round to the
Gunton-Cresswells's box to see what effect the act had
had on them. One glance at their faces was enough.
They were long and hard. "This is a real compliment,"
I said to myself, for the whole party cut me dead. I
withdrew, delighted. They had come, of course, to assist at my failure. I had often observed to Julian how
curiously lacking I was in dramatic instinct, and Julian
had predicted to Eva and her aunt and uncle a glorious
fiasco. They were furious at their hopes being so eg-
regiously disappointed. Had they dreamt of a success
they would have declined to be present. Indeed, half-
way through Act Two, I saw them creeping away into
the night.

The Barrel Club I discovered in the bar. As I ap-
proached, I heard Michael declare that "there'd not
been such an act produced since his show was put on
at——" He was interrupted by old Maundrell asserting
that "the business arranged for valet reminded him of
a story about Leopold Lewis."

They, too, added their quota to my cup of pleasure by being distinctly frigid.

Ascending to the gallery I found another compliment awaiting me. Tom Blake was fast asleep. The quality of Blake's intellect was in inverse ratio to that of Mrs. Goodwin. Neither of them appreciated the stuff that suited so well the tastes of the million; and it was consequently quite consistent that while Mrs. Goodwin dozed in spirit Tom Blake should snore in reality.

With Hatton and Price I did not come into contact. I noticed, however, that they wore an expression of relief at the enthusiastic reception my play had received.

But an encounter with Kit and Malim was altogether charming. They had had some slight quarrel on the way to the theatre, and had found a means of reconciliation in their mutual emotion at the pathos of the first act's finale. They were now sitting hand in hand telling each other how sorry they were. They congratulated me warmly.

A couple of hours more, and the curtain had fallen.

The roar, the frenzied scene, the picture of a vast audience, half-mad with excitement—how it all comes back to me.

And now, as I sit in this quiet smoking-room of a St. Peter's Port hotel, I hear again the shout of "Author!" I see myself again stepping forward from the wings. That short appearance of mine, that brief speech behind the footlights fixed my future. . . .

"James Orlebar Cloyster, the plutocratic playwright, to Margaret, only daughter of the late Eugene Grandison Goodwin, LL.D."

c 1

Wodehouse, Pelham Grenville, 1881-
      1975.
      Not George Washington : an autobi
   ographical novel / P. G. Wodehouse
   and Herbert Westbrook ; edited and
   introduced by David A. Jasen. -- Ne
   York : Continuum, 1980.
      x, 205 p. ; 22 cm.

      ISBN 0-8164-9349-9

      1. Westbrook, Herbert, joint
   author. I. Jasen, David A. II.
   Title.
PZ3.W817Nn 1980   823'.9'12
[PR6045.O53]

                                          79-2416
                                              MAR

Library of Congress
05850   PE   587138   B   © THE BAKER & TAYLOR CO.   022